I0822438

VOLUME ONE

BOOK ONE

THE ANCIENT BLOOD

BY

DWAYNE ANTHONY MADRY

Printed in the United States of America

First Printing, 2024

ISBN 978-1-963089-00-4

Cover Design by JessHavok

www.SAHAEL.com

Introduction

I want to congratulate you on purchasing this book, The Bloodlines of Sahael, Volume One, Book One: The Ancient Blood. As you read this work, you will come to see a complex story that tries to solve the mystery of humanity. It will take you on a roller coaster as you experience fresh and possibly unfamiliar emotions. This book will open your eyes to the cultures and differences within all people and how easily those differences can be seen as weaknesses.

I graduated from college with a degree in history. I have used my background to help provide authentic stories about various peoples and cultures in our world to advance the narrative of these books. This novel, and the volumes that follow, will help and teach you how to see things in a different light. I urge you to take your time as there is so much to enjoy. Let's get started, shall we?

Dwayne Madry

Dwayne A. Madry

Intoduction into Sahael

The tale of Sahael unfolds in a world scarred by the relentless march of oppression and the shadow of tyranny. Once a bastion of power and glory, Sahael now lies in ruins, its people crushed under the iron grip of Lord Commander Natas and his ruthless army. Enslaved, forgotten, and dispersed, the proud nation of Sahael teeters on the brink of oblivion, its legacy fading into distant memory.

Amidst the despair and darkness, a glimmer of hope emerges in the form of four young princesses, heirs to the ancient bloodline that still pulses with the strength of ages past. Unaware of their true heritage, these princesses harbor within them a growing power, a primal urge to reclaim the lost splendor of their homeland and defy the forces that seek to crush their spirit.

As they navigate a treacherous landscape rife with classism, racism, sexism, and xenophobia, these princesses are thrust into a crucible of trials and tribulations, where their very existence challenges the oppressive norms of society. Their journey is one of self-discovery, empowerment, and the unwavering resolve to rise above the shadows of their ancestors and reshape the destiny of their people.

The threat of ethnic cleansing looms large, casting a sinister shadow over the land. Should these warriors falter in their quest, the darkness heralded by Lord Natas will sweep across Aarde, plunging the world into eternal night and erasing all trace of hope and resistance.

In the hands of creator Dwayne Madry, the world of Sahael comes to life with a darkly fantastic tapestry woven from the threads of racial politics, brutality, magic, and suspense. For nearly two decades, Madry has crafted a realm where the echoes of history reverberate with the weight of destiny, where the clash of wills and the dance of power shape the fate of nations.

Step into the world of Sahael, where the spirits of the oppressed rise as one to challenge the chains of enslavement and forge a new future. Bear witness to a story of resilience, defiance, and the enduring strength of the human spirit as the people of Sahael unite in a daring bid to reclaim their freedom and defy the darkness that seeks to consume them.

The branches of the Marula Tree connect the ancient lineages of Sahael to the Alkebulan bloodlines, so that Sahael can produce unlimited resources for itself and Alkebulan as a whole. Peace to all.

A TIME BEFORE TIME…….

We center every aspect of Aardian culture on the Marula Tree. The Sahaelians, Hornans, and Egyptians revere the Tree of Life, and they recognize it as a symbol of unity used to connect Sahael to Egyptus. The symbol links the Tree to the glorious land of Alkebulan through cleansing and a ritual before the two great gatherings.

TABLE OF CONTENTS

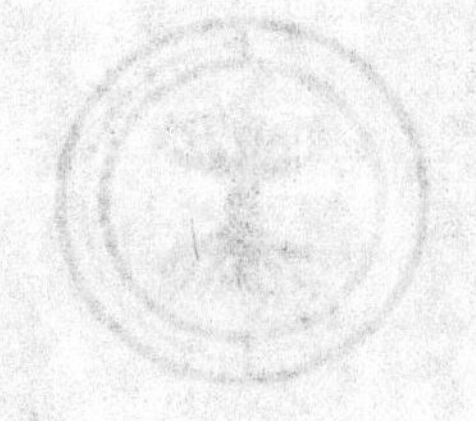

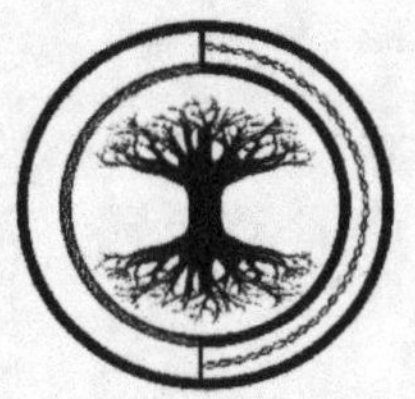

PART ONE: THE INVASION OF SAHAEL

KHARTOUM PALACE

It was nightfall. Orange-tinted flames charred the palace's ivory pillars, stretching toward the vaulted ceilings with a brightness that envied the moonlight. Black smoke filled the once-immaculate citadel, ripping the oxygen from its victims. Screams echoed from the city below as innocents suffered unspeakable cruelty.

The sun had risen for the last time on the Sahael of old. A long night of uncertainty and pain would follow.

Surrounded by fireflies lighting her path, High Queen Nergal raced through the grandiose chamber of Khartoum Palace at a full sprint. Her three-year-old daughter, Oadira, clung anxiously to her back as she held her nieces, Aamira and Heziara, in her arms. Despite being surrounded by death, the girls comprehended little of the crisis at hand beyond the anxiety of their protector.

High Queen Nergal reached the common area situated at the center of Khartoum Palace, where the four halls of the bloodlines converged. Her feet patted against the smooth tiles making almost no sound at all. Before proceeding, she abruptly slowed her pace, suspicious of what lurked before her. The

Navigators, guardians of the Medjay Gate, were nowhere to be found.

The hall was empty.

The Navigators would never abandon their posts…unless their lives had already been lost.

"Oopmaak!" the high queen yelled, voice echoing off the ornate carved ceilings high overhead. If the Navigators were gone, the Nabtahenge Gates would be descending into the sacred chamber at that very moment.

And so it was.

Nergal approached the massive marble gateway in the center of the hall, a series of tall, polished stones, twelve feet high, topped with identical stones all set in a circular pattern. Rock ground against tile, vibrating Nergal's teeth as the stone gate slowly descended into its protected housing below the palace. It would be safe there until summoned again by one with authority.

Nergal had the authority, but neither the time nor energy required to perform such an act.

No, her magics would be better used elsewhere. She had the girls to think of, and her sisters. Best to let the gate rest and not fall into Natas' possession.

It was too late for easy answers and quick escapes.

Nergal turned to the right toward the hidden ivory door adorned with the symbol of the Marula Tree. Her sapphire eyes glowed cerulean blue, triggering a sensation deep within her chest. The Orishan artes of Nergal's ancestors bloomed in her veins like an orchid. Adrenaline surged along with it, tingling in her flesh and extending to her fingertips. The mystic tattoos along her arms and shoulders began to glow pale blue as energy moved through her tall form. Vibrant colors of cobalt, indigo, green, and grayish white consumed the ivory door as it swung open, allowing her to enter her momentary sanctuary.

Her guard finally dropped as she entered the hidden chamber. Warmth from the fire kissed her skin but did nothing to thaw the frigid cold of her heart. Tapestries hung from the polished walls, hand-woven in bright colored threads, depicting Sahaelian triumphs from centuries past, along with written prophecies of Solomon and the Elder Seers.

The High Queen's fatigue began to get the best of her, so she kneeled to allow Oadira off her back while gently dropping the two girls onto the cold tile floor. She touched her daughter's face and ran her fingers through Oadira's dark hair with its hint of blue in the curls.

Queen Regent Arishkegal and Great Queen Ninti turned as Nergal released the children. The dark skin of their faces softened with relief at the sight of their fellow queen still protecting their daughters. They stepped forward, formal robes billowing as pieces of fine jewelry tinkled with their movements. Their regal arm and shoulder tattoos, similar in style to Nergal's, prickled with color in response to their apprehension. Ninti, a daughter of Aerokinesis, spread the bird-like wings that grew from her shoulder blades as she ran toward her daughter, Heziara. Gray and brown feathers encompassed the child as she embraced her mother. The young girl, whose own wings were still white and not yet strong enough to fly, wept in the embrace of her mother's warm plumage.

Aamira, green-tinted hair bouncing on her head, ran to Arishkegal in tears. Her face pressed firmly into their mother's bosoms; terrified words unintelligible through the layers of rich fabric that clothed her protectors.

"Sahael," Nergal exhaled, "is on fire. The Narsans and the Ennead have infiltrated Khartoum Palace. The Navigators are likely dead. Other than the girls and I, there will be no survivors. Natas will make sure of it. The capital city of Sahael falls tonight."

Arishkegal and Ninti looked at each other, no response to Nergal's words coming to their lips. After taking a moment to gather their thoughts, the queens wrapped their children in warm animal skins and let them rest on the pillows arranged around the fireplace. They then turned their royal attention to the surprise assault and potential end of their bloodline.

The queens sat down on low stools of intricately carved wood arranged in a half-circle before the small fire. Their muscles tensed beneath their dark, regal skin, straining against Nebiriau's golden bracelets that attached to their wrists. Each queen's bracelet was identical, save for a different colored stone at the center which matched the color of their eyes; blue sapphire for Nergal, green emerald for Arishkegal, and gray opal for Ninti. Stately ornaments of diamonds, rubies, and onyx adorned their robes, reflecting the meager light in the hidden room; each item of jewelry honoring their royal status.

"We, too, had to fight our way to get here," Queen Regent Arishkegal said. "I wounded a great deal of Narsans, but they still managed to kill all of my guards."

"The same happened to me," Ninti added. Her fierce, Hematite-gray-colored eyes beamed with power. Feathers ruffled along her wings like blades ready to slice their enemies. She slammed her hand against her leg as she spoke, muscular body, equal in height and strength to her fellow queens, radiating frustration. "The soldiers killed without a word! I sent many to the underworld, but when my husband heard the call of the other kings, I rushed here as tradition dictates."

"High Queen Nergal, what's our present situation?" Arishkegal asked.

Nergal paused. "Dire. Our bloodline may very well end tonight."

"No!" Ninti shouted. "What of Morrighan?"

Nergal waved toward an empty stool to their left. "The fourth seat is empty. Queen Morrighan and Princess Damisiah's whereabouts are unknown."

"I hope Morrighan got to her daughter in time, but what if she's…"

"Don't allow your mind to ponder such useless thoughts, Arishkegal. Our fellow queen is strong. I'm certain she managed to escape," Ninti asserted. "What about the four kings?"

"Yes! Our husbands. What happened to them?" Arishkegal added, looking at High Queen Nergal with a worried expression on her beautiful face.

"When the invasion finally reached the capital city of Sahael," Nergal began, glancing from her fellow queens toward the girls resting in their animal skin blankets, "our husbands were fighting at the river gates, which were breached by Tryton, Nata's personal flagship. I didn't see them until they came back to Khartoum." Her voice broke slightly, but she regained composure like the royal ruler she had been trained to be. "In the end, our husbands gave up their lives to give me the chance to escape with our daughters."

Silence engulfed the room. Nothing beyond the crackling of burning wood in the fireplace could be heard.

Arishkegal began to cry quietly as she played with the ring on her finger.

"How is that possible?" Ninti asked with heavy breathing.

The High Queen searched for words as sapphire tears slowly ran down her cheeks. "I'm not sure. The kings fought with great skill and power and yet . . . somehow . . .Natas's forces easily overwhelmed them. The strongest men in the realm were as but children before him. He defeated our husbands personally."

"During my altercation with them, I noticed an unusual

difference in strength," Arishkegal said, wiping her tears. "While some possessed the vigor one would expect from the Narsan and Ennead, the majority of Lord Commander Natas's forces had the same amount of power as we do. Others were even greater." Her voice dropped to little more than a whisper. "More disturbingly, their focus was not on seeking our husbands or us. They're in pursuit of our daughters."

"All of this? To get to our daughters?" Ninti responded, face blanched, eyes wide.

"Our girls are, after all, quite special," replied Arishkegal as she stared at the three young children lying before them. "Lord Commander Natas aims to divide our bloodlines. From the womb, our daughters have the power to unite nations. The girls are his greatest threat. He has accepted that truth, and now, so must we."

Suddenly, screams echoed somewhere inside the palace, slightly suffocated by the thick walls, yet close enough to gain the queens' attention. The little girls sat up, looking to their mothers for protection.

Ninti stood, knocking her stool to the floor with a clang of wood against tile. Her wings flapped as if she was ready to fly into battle at that very moment. "We are not safe here, even in our hidden chamber. Perhaps the gates will be kind and grant us safe passage through to other realms. With the proper incantations---"

"There's no time for speculation," Nergal interrupted. "We need to act with the knowledge we have. Natas did not plan this invasion over breakfast this morning. He knew what he was doing and how he would trap us. The Nabtahenge Gates have already pulled themselves back into the ground. The moment Khartoum Palace was breached, and the Navigators left their post to defend us, the stones retreated. I saw it with my own eyes as I entered the palace. Even if it were possible now to recall the stones, it would require too much of our magics, and we'd still need the

Navigators' assistance to get you to Nethal's realm, Arishkegal to Nero's, and myself to Nier's dominion."

"Is there nothing we can do to save our girls?" Arishkegal inquired, lowering her head to her chest in defeat.

Ninti's eyes widened, as if an idea gave her hope. "If they aren't already dead, it's possible that the Navigators went into exile for their own safety, but . . ."

"But Sahael is now isolated from everyone," the Great Queen interjected, gritting her teeth. "It doesn't matter where the Navigators are. If they are not here in this palace, we are indeed truly alone."

"We need to pray for assistance from our gods," Great Queen Ninti responded, dropping to her knees immediately.

"So say we all," the other two echoed, also kneeling beside the stools.

"Girls," Nergal said, holding out her hand to Oadira. "Join us in supplication."

The little ones took their mother's hands, and they all lowered their heads to offer a prayer to Obatala and Ishtar for guidance.

Speaking simultaneously, they prayed, "Our great Sahaelian parents, who are among us, we humbly offer our thanks for the many blessings you have given. We extend our love to the land's ultimate state of wellbeing for the suffering that you endured so that we may know peace and solace. As the mother and father of our great Sahaelian souls, we beseech you to further lead and guide us to higher understanding, to lead us to our true greatness, with a more encompassing dedication of love for our Sahaelian subjects. We ask thee, the parents of all Sahaelians and Alkebulans, to guide us toward greater unity. Give us strength to become stronger in our communal family structure. We raise our heads high, asking for strength, guidance, and direction from the architects, our creators, and the gods. With our heads high, we seek inspiration through our heritage and legacy that you have left us to uphold and sustain. The rightful existence of all Sahaelians and Alkebulan people will be wiped out without your intervention."

A steep silence fell upon the room after the three queens finished offering their solemn prayer to Obatala and Ishtar. High Queen Nergal, Great Queen Ninti, and Queen Regent Arishkegal made eye contact with each other, feeling deep uneasiness with no answers, just tough choices about how their daughters would survive.

"Oadira," Nergal said. "You, Heziara and Aamira sit next to the fire while we queens discuss some difficult things. Understood?"

"Yes, Mama," Oadira nodded. Her eyes were every bit as blue as her mother's.

The queens retreated from the fire and walked toward the center of the room, closer to the secret entrance.

"I haven't received any impressions," Ninti said, scowling.

"Neither have I," Arishkegal said, looking up at the ceiling.

"I've received an impression of a burning within my heart!" Nergal exclaimed, jumping to check the enchantments on the sealed doors behind them. "Before I share my thoughts, is it possible you, High Queen Ninti, can fly the girls out of here and safely get them to the ships!"

"That won't work!" Arishkegal said. "Lord Commander Natas will have placed wind lances outside of Khartoum Palace just in case of an escape attempt of this type. It is a basic strategy. They'd kill you and the girls instantly."

"Not only that," Ninti whispered. "But I couldn't carry all three girls. Two perhaps, but not three. I wouldn't be able to fly for long, or very high, while carrying all of them. We would most certainly be slain."

More muffled screams could be heard through the hidden door.

"I feared this," High Queen Nergal said candidly. "I hoped to come up with a different plan than what my heart tells me, but it is not to be. For our daughters to safely escape, we may have to place them in harm's way, and ourselves on the path of the dead."

"What do you mean?" Arishkegal asked, looking over at the girls as firelight danced around their small silhouettes.

Nergal did the same, focusing on Oadira's cerulean irises reflecting the light of the fire. "Let us speak in silence for a moment, as is the way of the Queen."

Opening her mind, Nergal connected to the thoughts of her sisters, feeling their emotions, and seeing past the emotional barriers they currently employed to keep from feeling pain and fear. Much like Nergal, their thoughts were a jumble of anxiety, anger, and deep-seeded grief.

"We must cast a spell altering the children's eyes and thus concealing their true identities." Nergal spoke directly to their minds. She and Ninti had always been the most skilled at this arte, while Arishkegal had excelled at feeling the emotions of animals. The telepathy itself was a closely guarded secret among the royal family, one Nergal planned to keep to her dying breath, which may come sooner than she wished. *"This spell,"* she continued, *"will last for decades if needed, allowing our daughters to possess features similar to Alkebulan children. Once we have performed our artes, we'll bring our daughters to the slave ports."*

"Slave ports? Have you lost your mind!" Ninti yelled telepathically. *"Better for them to die with us then spend their lives in slavery!"*

"No," replied High Queen Nergal as she stared at Arishkegal and Ninti. *"As normal girls, they'll blend in at the slave ports alongside the other Alkebulan children. This way, our girls can evade Lord Commander Natas's grasp entirely."*

Ninti stood, tattoos glowing as rage flooded her veins. *"I'd rather fight and die than allow our daughters to serve as slaves or be sold for their feminine virtues! They were chosen and blessed by Ishtar and Obatala."*

"Their fate would be worse than death!" Arishkegal agreed, standing in front of her daughter like a shield.

"The chance of them being molested at their age is unlikely," Nergal said.

Great Queen Ninti cringed, wings pulling close to her body. *"Yet, the possibility still exists!"*

"Their lives would mean nothing as slaves," Queen Regent Arishkegal added.

"Nothing!" Ninti shouted into her sister's minds. *"I will die here and now beside my daughter before they spend their lives as field hands and future bed wenches."*

"I understand!" High Queen Nergal said, raising her hand to cut off Ninti and Arishkegal's protests. *"I understand your concerns, but keep in mind that Nebiriau's bracelets will provide them with protection if we employ the proper spells. With our magics, we can guarantee they will be protected by the Gods. It is no small thing I ask of you, my sisters, but if you would rather die than see them slaves, we can die now, the three of us, and they can live under divine protection until they are able to stand on their own. Our lives in exchange for theirs."*

Great Queen Ninti stepped toward her fellow queen. *"What are you proposing?"*

"A holy sacrifice," replied Nergal.

"What type of sacrifice?" Arishkegal asked.

The secret room grew quiet except for the continued screams of death and gore spilling to the ground by the Nabtahenge Gates. The foul smell of iron and blood seeped through the seams in the wall.

High Queen Nergal pointed toward the hidden door with passionate enthusiasm, breaking the mental connection with her fellow queens. "Our people—men and women, young and old—are being slaughtered," she spoke out loud for all to hear. "Lord Commander Natas, the Narsans, and the Ennead Legion are here to not only massacre every royal member of the Ancient Bloodline; they're here to annihilate our people and erase us from history!"

"To save our daughters, we would do anything," Arishkegal began slowly. "What would be required of us?"

Nergal, face as hard as stone, took a deep breath before replying. "You know the sacrifice. *We* are the sacrifice; you, Ninti, and myself. Our life energies will fill Nebiriau's bracelets, and Njiru's rings will act as barriers, ensuring the children are not harmed. When someone seeks to hurt them, the magics will influence the predator's minds to move along. Others unfortunately will take our daughters' places as a sacrifice for the greater good of Aarde. And if we make their eyes normal like average Alkebulans, our girls will be protected from the worst of a slave's fate. When the magic is no more, a deep yearning will spring up within them and call our children home."

"So, they will have brown eyes allowing them to blend in?" asked Arishkegal, deep concern in her voice.

"Yes," replied Nergal without further elaboration. "Thoughts, my sisters?"

"How do you expect to accomplish all of this and get us all out of here?" asked Ninti.

“It will begin with me. I’ll hold off Lord Commander Natas’s armies for as long as possible. Use that time to escape with our daughters. My sacrifice will act as the first barrier. Your death will become the second and third, and the fourth for Queen Morrighan. I will try to communicate our plan to her telepathically…if she is still in-tune…and alive. As the five of you move further away from me, my magic will wither, but you will be protected until you are outside the palace’s gates.”

Again, nothing but the crackle of the fire could be heard. Even the screams had stopped.

“Keep in mind that if the four kings and queens die,” Nergal continued. “Khartoum Palace’s secondary defenses will activate, forcing anyone and anything outside the capital. The very air of Sahael will become toxic. Everything in the sacred land will die. But the promises have been made as well of life after this one, and for some in the chosen cities, a return to life during the chosen reclamation. Let us have faith in the words of the prophets.”

“Is there a way out of this room without being discovered?” Arishkegal asked. “You are the keeper of the secrets, High Queen.”

Nergal pointed toward the hot coals on the hearth. “When you are ready to leave, once the first sacrifice has been made, remove the poker, and a set of stairs will reveal themselves. The sewer tunnels will lead you into the forest.”

High Queen Nergal sat back down with Great Queen Ninti and Queen Regent Arishkegal. The little girls continued their silent vigil over the fire, unaware of the import of their mothers’ conversation.

“Oadira, please come here,” Nergal said, motioning for her daughter to sit with her. “I’d like to speak with you for a moment.”

Oadira did as instructed and sat down beside her mother.

Her dark skin glistened in the firelight.

Nergal quickly took off her ornate golden bracelet and placed it around Oadira's left wrist. She then removed one of the rings from her pinky and slid it onto Oadira's index finger. Arishkegal and Ninti called their daughters over and mimicked Nergal's instructions to Oadira, giving their bracelet and a ring to their little children.

Swallowing the rigid lump in her throat, Nergal placed Oadira's right hand on the piece of jewelry. "Your father gave me this bracelet prior to your birth. He said its wearer takes life or gives their life for the one they love, allowing their spiritual essence to transfer into the bracelet. Their spirit will then be able to watch over its new wearer forever."

High Queen Nergal stood and carried Oadira away from the others. She sat against the wall behind a tapestry depicting the creation of Sahael. Sapphire tears ran down her cheeks.

Speaking an ancient incantation, Nergal's tattoos glowed blue. The air in her right hand became solid matter as the High Queen conjured a ceremonial knife with a sapphire handle and rubies in the hilt. She placed it in Oadira's hand. Nergal then gently placed both her own hands on her daughter's cheeks and touched their foreheads together.

"My dear Oadira," the Queen began. "What I'm about to request from you is for your protection and the survival of the Orishan bloodline. No matter the cost, you must get to the slave port."

Oadira looked at her mother with a blank stare, eyes moistened by fear and confusion.

"Use this knife to end my life," High Queen Nergal requested. "This will instill my essence in Nebiriau's bracelet, along with your father's ring, guiding you out of Khartoum Palace.

Do you understand?"

"Yes, Mama," replied Oadira with a trembling lip.

"Be brave now, my sweet Oadira," Nergal whispered.

Gently, the High Queen guided Oadira's hand and placed the knife against her throat.

"Do it, Oadira of Sahael. Allow my life to protect you now and always. Be strong and obedient, and remember, I will always be with you." A look of peace flowing across Nergal's face. "I will always be with you. Say it."

"You will always be with me," Oadira repeated.

Oadira's hand trembled under the guidance of her mother's. With one swift motion, Nergal forced Oadira's hand forward. The blade cut through the carotid artery and jugular vein of her mother's throat.

High Queen Nergal's eyes flew wide, but a smile pulled at her lips. Blood flowed freely from the wound, dripping into the bracelet around Oadira's wrist. Nergal raised her hand to the wound, magic from the queen's Ancient Bloodline radiating from the thick, red liquid. Tattoos glowed blue as tendrils of energy twisted from her fingers and slowed the blood flow.

"We have but moments," Arishkegal said, placing her hand on Oadira's shoulder. "She has slowed the loss of her sacred blood long enough to afford our escape. Come, child."

The conjured knife dropped from Oadira's hand. It clattered on the stone floor, echoing through the chamber, and then vanished. Blood continued pouring from High Queen Nergal's neck, but with less force than before. It trickled down her arms and dripped from her fingertips into a pool on the floor.

"Proud . . ." Nergal choked.

Oadira wept as she dropped to her knees into her mother's

pooling blood.

High Queen Nergal's bright, sapphire eyes and radiant tattoos dimmed as her essence departed, making its way into Nebiriau's ancient Kemettian bracelet.

Ninti placed her hand on High Queen Nergal's slumping shoulders. "When the time comes, Queen Regent Arishkegal and I will be ready to do our part, High Queen. We'll safely smuggle the girls onto one of the slave ships resting on Lake Sahael. We will live to honor your sacrifice."

A voice echoed suddenly through the room. *"Life magic will keep me alive long enough to help you all get to safety."* It was Nergal's voice, though emanating from the air itself and not her severed vocal cords. *"Go now. I will remain and make my last stand against Natas. May the God's of Sahael protect you."*

Quiet sobbing filled the room. All three of the girls were crying, not understanding why the High Queen sat bleeding before them. Arishkegal flashed a sad smile to her daughter Aamira, who anxiously searched her mother's face for answers.

"Are the sewer tunnels safe, or have they been discovered by the Narsans and their Mastiff dogs?" Ninti asked.

"My ability to see through the eyes of sea creatures will not help us at this point," Nergal's voice resounded. *"But you, Ninti, can communicate with the fowl of the air. Call upon your Hausan abilities of interspecies communication."*

Closing her eyes, Ninti reached out to all life around her. She felt the insects scurrying between the palace walls, the Narsans plunging their swords into captives along the outer parapets, the dogs licking at spilled blood pooling beside the great fountain of Khartoum in the courtyard. The birds called to her though, creating a connection far more powerful than that of other creatures. Ninti reached further, seeing the outside of Khartoum Palace from above, smelled the fires and the stench of death. A hawk cried in her ears, but it wasn't a hawks' cry, it was her cry. She was the hawk, and the hawk Ninti. She felt its talons clutching a fish it had plucked from the water. The bird's confusion and pain engulfed her at the sight of Khartoum Palace burning. Its keen eyes saw all; the Narsan soldiers, and the Ennead Legion below.

The carnage was breathtaking.

Lope Mastiffs, dogs as large as horses, sniffed the area and ran down villagers hiding in trees or underneath bushes. Razor fangs mauled innocents while guttural growls echoed amidst screams.

Soldiers charged forward, killing anyone they came across without a word. No prisoners had been taken. No demands were issued.

And through the smoke and fumes she saw him: Lord Commander Natas with his piercing, wretched red eyes. He stood seven feet tall with long, dreadlocked hair, skin as dark as cocoa beans, pronounced cheekbones, and an angular chin. A large scarlet cloak draped over his maroon and obsidian-plated armor. Much like the queens, Natas' arms and shoulders were marked with intricate tribal tattoos, but where Ninti's glowed gray, Natas' glowed crimson, the color of sacrifice. Natas desecrated that color though, as the sacrifices he was interested in were never his own. Possessing a sturdy, thick, chiseled athletic frame, Natas used the dark artes of Khalidah to conjure two obsidian, arcane Topke Liganda longswords that he used in that moment to behead two palace guards Ninti had known for over 20 years.

Instinctively, the hawk understood evil and flew higher to escape any errant glance from the wicked invader. Before the hawk broke contact with Ninti, she saw the Ennead Legion rapidly closing in and creating a perimeter around Khartoum Palace. At the last second, Ninti felt Natas' aura focus on her. He looked up at the hawk and smiled.

Her eyes opened again to the hidden room with its tapestries and fireplace.

"Natas knows we're here!" Ninti breathed. "He felt my aura. He's coming."

"Are the tunnels clear?" Arishkegal asked.

"I didn't see anyone near the hidden exits along the forest side."

"The secret entrance by the fireplace will lead everyone to the outside walls of the palace," Nergal's disembodied voice ordered. *"If the tunnels are clear, it is your best chance. There are stairs below where the fire sits. Use them to get our daughters to safety."*

Queen Regent Arishkegal accessed the stairs by pulling on the poker attached to the grate below the flames. Gears groaned, and the stones along the wall pulled away from the fireplace, revealing steps to a dark lower level. Kicking the firewood aside hastily, Arishkegal coughed as smoke filled the room.

High Queen Nergal let out a heavy exhale as she stood with her shoulders back and head high. Blood continued trickling onto her cream-colored robes, leaving them smeared in red.

Her sacrifice would have meaning, unlike the sacrifices Natas demanded.

"Go now," Nergal said softly. Sapphire tears trickled down from her dimming blue eyes. *"Remember to touch the blood to the bracelets when your time arrives. Your sacrifices shall echo through the ages, my sisters. I'll hold on for as long as I can and hope that it is all the time you need. And if the Gods grant me justice, perhaps I will avenge myself of Natas by cutting a single hair from his head. Even that would be enough."*

“Let’s go!” Ninti said as she assumed command.

Arishkegal lifted Aamira and placed her on her back, while Ninti held on tight to Oadira and placed Heziara on her back. The five of them hurried down the stairs under the fireplace and never looked back.

High Queen Nergal, alone and dying, gained solace in knowing that her magic would protect Oadira. The secret entrance to the room rumbled behind her.

Natas had arrived.

The enchantments would not hold him back for long. She conjured a sapphire blade in her hand and turned to face her assailants. Many of them would be sent to Egyptus before she joined them in death.

In the catacombs under Khartoum Palace, Ninti and Arishkegal lead the princesses through the complex sewer system. The stench of human waste assaulted their senses, but at least in the almost complete darkness they couldn’t see the viscous muck that mired their queenly robes. Stone walls curved in an oval shape around them, just large enough for an ordinary man or woman to stand. At their heights though, the queens had to hunch. A stream of murky fluid ran beside a narrow walkway, emitting a smell like rotting meat on a summer afternoon. Darkness enveloped them, except for the glow from their tattoos.

“I can hear footsteps above us,” Ninti whispered. She gagged on the stench but continued running.

“Be careful in the darkness,” Arishkegal said. “Don’t go too fast.”

A rat squeaked somewhere in front of them. Oadira clawed at Arishkegal’s robes in response to the sound.

“It’s okay, little one. Follow the rats,” Arishkegal assured. “My Yoruban abilities allow me to feel their emotions. They’ll lead us out of here safely. They know the way. The rats flee Natas the same as all living creatures should."

"I will guide us forward," Ninti assured as she spoke a quick incantation to invoke her Hausan abilities. Her eyes lit up with a gray glow. Details of the sewer walls took shape, and everything became clear as a sunny afternoon. Up ahead Ninti noticed thin glowing strands stretching across the width of the sewers, like golden threads.

"There is a little light down here," Arishkegal said as she felt something pull against her outstretched hand and then give way slowly. "What is this substance I'm feeling?"

"Ouch!" Princess Aamira yelled, her voice echoing down the tunnel.

"What happened?" Arishkegal asked.

"Something bit me," Aamira whimpered.

"They are Aranak webs!" Ninti cried as her left wing snagged one of the sticky threads.

Arishkegal looked up and noticed webbing along the sewer walls. Tiny spiders crawled over wrapped rat carcasses and foul shapes undulated in the shadows.

"There are Aranak spiders everywhere," Ninti said. "I can see them all around. Stay close. Their poison is a mild irritation, but many bites will eventually overcome you."

Oadira retched at the pungent odor of sewage and the sight of the spiders. Marble-sized egg sacks hung from webs along the walls, and arachnids feasted on cockroaches and feces. Occasionally they would hear the crunching of spiders beneath their feet as they walked.

"We're almost there. I can smell the fresh air," Arishkegal said as a pale light took shape in the distance.

"We made it!" Ninti breathed.

The oppression of the sewers' darkness retreated as they entered a grove of trees next to a pool on the east side of Khartoum Palace. The sweet forest smells lifted their spirits as the moon shone brightly. Stars blinked above, obscured at times by the smoke blowing on the breeze.

"Take a moment to rest and clean yourselves in the water," Ninti ordered. "But we can't risk more than a moment or two before we continue our escape."

The tired girls wiped feces from their shoes in the pond while Arishkegal caught her breath. Orange-yellow fish stared up at them from the water's depths with shining blue eyes. Oadira cleaned her mother's blood from her fingers, seeing stains of red on her nightdress.

A wind blew warm suddenly from the direction of the palace. A voice echoed in the breeze, buoying their spirits. High Queen Nergal's presence suddenly radiated like pollen from a spring meadow in full bloom.

"Go, my love," the voice whispered. *"I will watch over you. I will always be close…"*

Oadira felt her mother's love as it filled the grove. The feeling retreated quickly like a candle blowing out in the wind.

Somewhere in the hidden rooms of Khartoum Palace, Nergal had perished.

"We need to keep moving," Arishkegal said, grabbing Aamira and Oadira from the bank of the pool. "The Sahaelian forest is our best option. It's thick and hard to travel through; it will take our pursuers a considerable amount of time to find us."

Ninti picked up Heziara and the group charged into the woods. The light of the moon acted as their only illumination. Hidden animals called out in the night, watching the queens and princesses on their flight. After a half hour of running, Arishkegal gasped, lowered the girls, and slumped over with both hands on her waist. She breathed heavily. Emerald-colored sweat trickled down her forehead and cheeks.

"We must rest," Arishkegal gasped.

"Only for a moment," Ninti said through deep breaths of her own.

Suddenly, a series of loud booms rolled through the forest. Crickets went silent in response. A deer darted through the trees away from the sound.

"Do you hear that?" Arishkegal asked as she gripped the girls tighter to her body.

"Obsidian nitrate bombs," Ninti whispered.

The distant bombardment continued for the next few minutes. At one point, Ninti accessed her Yoruban sight, seeing through the wind and elements; feeling the emotion of even the plants and flowers. The earth shook as bombs dropped from Narsan floating airships. The walls of Khartoum Palace crumbled. Fire burned the tapestries in the secret chambers, destroying the very history of Sahael. She felt the grass under Natas' feet as he watched the citadel explode under his nitrate onslaught.

"Check the perimeter around the palace." The malice behind Lord Commander Natas's words could not be misinterpreted, even though Ninti stood miles away in the forest. Natas wiped blood from his palms on a piece of cloth. Strands of emotion touched the fabric and Ninti knew it was a fragment of Nergal's robes. The blood was Nergal's as well. Natas had taken both as a macabre trophy.

"Destroy all that remains of this filthy palace," Natas continued. "Send the Ennead Legion into the forest to search for the queens. They couldn't have gotten far! The High Queen has already joined her husband in the afterlife. The Queen Regent, Great Queen, and the princesses will soon follow."

"Yes, my lord," the soldiers shouted in response.

"Release the Lope Mastiffs to track them down if they went into the forest." Natas turned toward the east and pointed. "Where is Nassir's sapphire obelisk? I want to destroy and curse it so the water in the city of Sahael can never return no matter what magics Solomon or anyone else tries to use! Shatter the stone! Burn it all!"

Ninti broke her connection with the emotions of the land, no longer wanting to feel the pain of Natas' attack, nor the apathy dripping from his every word.

"Hurry! There's little time," she warned.

Queen Regent Arishkegal reluctantly let a few emerald tears run down her cheeks as Aamira cried softly in her lap.

"Our tears will do us no good, young Aamira," Arishkegal said, wiping her daughter's face. "Now is the time for strength and speed." She stood, turning toward Ninti and Heziara as they leaned against a great oak tree. "What did you see?"

"Lord Commander Natas is releasing his Lope Mastiffs into the forest to hunt us down," Ninti replied. "I saw it with my Yoruban Sight. We cannot outrun them. We must find transportation or somewhere to hide, or we'll never make it to the port."

Arishkegal nodded and stood back up straight. "I'll communicate with the creatures of the forest. I'll ask for aid."

Closing her eyes, Arishkegal felt the awareness of the woodland open to her senses. She asked any animals, large or small, to help her find somewhere safe where they could hide. The moment passed quickly and felt insufficient, yet dozens of squirrels approached the women, tiny eyes lighting up with Queen Regent Arishkegal's emerald energy.

"Where do we go?" asked Ninti.

"Over there," Arishkegal pointed, voice exhausted.

The animals led the fleeing group to a large cave that could momentarily serve as a respite. They cautiously entered the cavern, walking past a large boulder on their right. The mothers put their children down as soon as they could and rested. Two platypuses waddled from the darkness, making eye contact with Arishkegal before leaving the cave immediately. The animals began covering their tracks with their large tails, swiping and moving back and forth through the dust to ensure that Lord Commander Natas, the Narsans, and the Ennead Legion could not follow them.

Murky darkness enveloped the women as they settled into the cave. Water dripped with quiet echoes deeper in the fissure. The scent of decay lingered in the stale air. Queen Regent Arishkegal stepped forward into the darkness, feeling old bones shift beneath her feet.

"What is this place?" Great Queen Ninti asked, looking around, trying to picture where she was.

"A bear's cave," Arishkegal replied.

"Bears!" whispered Ninti, peering into the darkness in search of movement.

"Untamed Sahaelian bears live here," Arishkegal said. "We can rest safely for a bit. The squirrels tell me they aren't here right now; using the night for their hunting."

"We need to keep moving," Ninti urged.

"We can't keep going at the speed we have. We'll collapse from exhaustion before we reach the ships. The girls need to eat and rest as well. It's too dangerous to continue traveling on foot,"

Arishkegal sat beside her daughter and breathed deeply. Hundreds of tiny emerald eyes appeared suddenly from the mouth of the cave, squeaking and rustling through the dry leaves and bones littering the cave floor. “I’ve communicated with the squirrels,” Arishkegal said, leaning against the rocky wall and closing her eyes. “They’ve scavenged some food for us. I’ll keep watch for Lord Commander Natas, the Narsans, and his Ennead commanders through the eyes of the forest. For now, let’s use this time to rest, eat, and keep the girls protected.”

Ninti wrapped her wings around the girls to help conserve warmth in the cold cave. They all snuggled close, quietly listening for their enemies.

Hours passed in the silent forest. The princesses slept while Ninti and Arishkegal took turns keeping watch. Slowly, the pale light of dawn approached, adding a slight gray hue to the cave’s mouth.

Something grunted at the cavern’s entrance. Large paws thumped against the dirt followed by sniffing and a low growl.

Arishkegal nudged Ninti awake. Several eight-foot-tall, pale white bears lumbered into the cave from the ashen light of dawn. A strong pine scent filled the space, along with the musk of wet fur. Arishkegal opened her Yoruban senses to communicate with the creatures. They were confused by the presence of humans in their den. The bears had run from other humans searching the forest to the north. Smoke had obscured the scent of berries in the wood and forced the bears to abandon their search for food.

“Mama?” Aamira whispered. Arishkegal glanced down at her daughter as the girl looked curiously up at the enormous bears. Aamira’s emerald eyes grew wide in fascination, not fear. She fearlessly stepped forward and reached up toward one of the two-thousand-pound behemoths. Arishkegal wanted to pull her daughter away from the bears but knew such a sudden movement might spook the beasts. For their part, the bears seemed more curious than frightened of the tiny child. The closest Sahaelian bear bowed its head toward Aamira and sniffed. Aamira rubbed behind the bear's ear.

Arishkegal then recognized the beast and smiled sadly.

Ninti's heart pounded in her chest. Sweat dripped from her upper lip and the feathers on her wings twitched nervously. "We must leave. Now!"

"I've communicated with the bears," Arishkegal said. "They are afraid of the dangers in the forest. They've seen Ennead soldiers and Lope Mastiffs are in the woods to the north. But we are safe. This is alpha bear is Olami, my husband Enqi's chosen battle mount. He was wounded in the battle and has sought us out on orders from my husband…before he perished."

"Are you serious?" Great Queen Ninti questioned.

"They tell me that at the far end of the cave there's another exit," Arishkegal said. "They can lead us there."

"Will they aid us?" Ninti asked.

"With enough concentration, I'll be able to subdue their fear instinct, and you can ride them to the ports," Arishkegal said. "Olami is well trained. He will protect our daughters with his own life, just as my husband would have.

"Are you sure?" Great Queen Ninti questioned. "I will not go alone. We will travel together."

Arishkegal shook her head. "Great Queen Ninti, it's time. I'll seal off the cavern and distract the Lope Mastiffs and their Ennead masters. I will try to influence the dogs with my abilities, but they are well trained in their hate. The Lope Mastiffs won't stop hunting for more than a moment. Mount the bears and escape with the girls."

"Isn't there another way?" Ninti asked as tears fell from her eyes. "We've lost so much tonight. I know we talked of sacrifice, but perhaps---"

"It's the only way," Arishkegal interrupted. "Nergal's death, and those of our beloved husbands, will not be in vain. I will stand inside this cave and draw Natas's army's attention. I will collapse the cave on top of them and myself if I have to." Arishkegal grabbed Ninti's arms tightly. "These three princesses are now your responsibility; we have little time."

Several squirrels scratched at Arishkegal's feet, squeaking loudly. "The Ennead are drawing nearer," she said. "All life in the forest is afraid. The time for my sacrifice has arrived. My life force will ensure the survival and protection of our daughters. We knew we would not survive this journey. We're the sacrifice. Your choice will come soon enough."

Aamira grabbed her mother's hand as tears flowed down her beautiful, ebony face.

"No need to cry, little one," Queen Regent Arishkegal said in a soothing voice as she hugged her little girl tight. She wiped the silent tears from Aamira's cheeks and wondered if her little angel would remember her. She brought her forehead to her daughter's and closed her eyes tight. "What I'm about to ask you to do will be the hardest thing you'll ever do."

Just like Nergal had in the secret chamber of Khartoum Palace, Arishkegal used her Yoruban artes and slowly conjured a decorative jade knife.

"Take this blade," she instructed. "I need you to cut the large vein on my inner leg just as Oadira cut her mother's arteries on her neck. I do not have the strength of Nergal to survive cutting my throat. This wound will allow me to bleed out slowly while I pass my protective power onto your bracelet. It will also give me enough time to send animals in different directions to confuse our enemies. You need to get away from Lord Commander Natas. I have the strongest connection with the alpha bear. His name is Olami. He was your father's mount, wounded in the battle. He found his way to us and will now be your mount, my sweet child."

Aamira nodded. With the help of her mother, the green knife pierced the flesh of Arishkegal's leg, cutting the woman's saphenous vein on her inner thigh.

A small puddle of blood formed on the floor beneath the Queen Regent. Dark crimson seeped into the ground and the cracks in the rocks. Arishkegal dipped her fingers into the blood and raised them over the bracelet on Aamira's wrist. Warm red liquid dripped onto the piece of jewelry in tiny round spots.

"Now let my strength be yours, Daughter of Sahael," Arishkegal spoke softly.

Aamira cried uncontrollably as she watched the spirit of life slowly leave her mother's body and enter the bracelet on her arm. The glowing green tattoos on the Queen's biceps faded along with her protective power.

After a moment, Arishkegal looked up at Ninti, face pale but confident. "Go, my sister. Get them to the boats. Let our strength protect them. Trust in our land and the Gods of our ancestors. Sahael will rise once more. Natas will not triumph for long."

Ninti touched her forehead to the dying Queen Regent's before loading the three girls on Olami's massive back. They gripped tightly to his short white fur and shifted so they could all fit. Ninti climbed on behind the girls to make sure they didn't fall off or lose their grip during the flight through the forest. Olami growled softly and stamped his massive feet.

Arishkegal touched the beast's paw and nodded. "Go. Keep our daughters as safe as you would your own cub."

With a deep snort, Olami took off into the cave's depths.

"Oadira! Aamira! Heziara! Firmly hold onto each other," Ninti urged as the wind blew through her hair.

Light pierced their eyes suddenly as the bear exited the cave into the morning sun. Ninti looked around the vast forest as many animal species—pumas, lions, tigers, elephants, hippos, and giraffes—stood guard over the young princesses. Birds circled overhead, crying out as if to goad the bear to move faster. Arishkegal's power seemed to spread, calling on all wildlife to come to their defense.

Howls of Lope Mastiffs echoed behind them. Olami jumped over a large log and jostled the riders. Growls and cries tore through the forest as the Mastiffs met resistance from the other gathered animals and the thickness of the forest. Ninti didn't look back as Olami loped up a steep area in the Sahaelian forest. Branches clawed at their skin as the bear darted through a bush. One of the girls cried out and grabbed at her arm, where blood dripped from where a thorn had torn the skin. The bear continued running as if the Mastiffs were directly behind him. They reached the crest of the hill and began descending. A large body of water teeming with fish appeared through the Marula Trees below.

It was Lake Sahael.

"When we emerge from this forest, there will be a clearing that overlooks a large body of water." Ninti said to the girls, using her Hausan telepathy so as not to catch the keen ears of the Mastiffs chasing them. *"We'll have to jump in the lake, or else we won't make it. It's the only way to avoid being caught."*

Ninti sensed the girls' fear. They were strong princesses, but too young to be experiencing the darkness of the past night.

The daughters nodded their heads in agreement, though their faces still registered terror. Olami ran alongside the southern end of the lake, climbing a rocky outcropping 40 feet above the water below. There was no time for the queen and her charges to ease into the jump.

It was now or never.

"On the count of three," Great Queen Ninti said telepathically, *"we'll jump off this cliff. Olami will draw them away from us. One, two, three! Jump!"*

She wrapped her arms around the three girls, and they leaped off Olami's back together. Olami veered to the left and made his way back down the cliff as the girls fell. The world tumbled around them, air buffeting their faces. Ninti spread her wings to slow their descent and make sure they didn't hurt themselves on impact. Each second of the fall felt like an hour. Finally, the cold water took their breath away as they hit the surface and plunged beneath.

Air filled their lungs once more as they broke the lake's surface. Ninti made sure all three princesses were alright before they started dog paddling in the freshwater toward the shoreline.

Otters suddenly flanked them in the water and pressed themselves against the girls to help them swim the rest of the way.

Ninti smiled. Arishkegal was still alive, still communicating with the animals to help them. What a strong queen. There would never be another like her and Nergal, not until Sahael was reborn for future generations.

"Follow the flow of the current leading toward Lake Sahael," she communicated to the girls. *"Queen Arishkegal still lives and is helping us. Thank the Gods of Sahael for her sacrifice. Look forward, daughters. Avoid hitting the large rock structures protruding out of the water."*

The three tiny princesses held onto the otters, resting their arms and legs. Cold water bit their fingers and toes, but they no longer heard the barking of Mastiffs or smelled smoke from burning palaces. Masts and sails took shape through a pale morning mist in the distance, alerting Ninti of their proximity to the slave ships.

"*We're close*," Ninti said, urging the otters toward the shore.

Warmer water surrounded them as they reached the shallows. The otters helped the exhausted girls to dry land before disappearing below the lake's surface, taking the echo of Queen Arishkegal's love with them.

"Follow me," Ninti said out loud, grabbing Heziara's hand and waving to Oadira and Aamira to keep up as they ran toward a meadow of tall grass. "The slave port is several kilometers away still. Stay close."

Wet and cold, Heziara pulled her young wings close to her body in an attempt to keep warm.

Lope Mastiff howls echoed from the tree line on the far side of the lake.

"Kak!" Ninti swore. "They must've caught onto our scent. Heziara, climb onto my back," she ordered while grabbing Oadira and Aamira in her arms. The queen raced through the grass at full speed. Her muscular legs burned like they never had before in her life. Flying would be so much easier, but she couldn't carry all three girls and maintain her altitude. Plus, their plan required secrecy. A flying Sahaelian Queen would draw plenty of attention. She wanted nothing more than to stop running, lie down and let her body rest, but she knew if she did so, the princesses would be taken.

She would never let that happen. They had sacrificed too

much at this point to fail in their mission.

And the sacrifice was not yet complete.

Soon Ninti would join her sisters and trust their daughters to the protection of the Gods of Sahael.

After ten minutes of marathon running, they arrived at the edge of the Sahaelian docks where the freighters and slave ships moored. The royal family had long sought to destroy the slavers and their ships, but the captains of these wretched vessels always seemed to slip through their grasp and find other ways of exploiting the poor and disadvantaged. Seeing the ships now with their white sails, pretending to be pure and clean, made Ninti want to set fire to the entire fleet.

Unfortunately, it seemed the Narsans had arrived long before Ninti and the girls.

Gazing out from behind a Marula Tree, Ninti watched dozens of Narsan soldiers harassing slaves lined up like cattle waiting to board the ships. Large Lope Mastiffs sniffed and growled at the depressing mass of people, barking loudly. Natas's forces stood at attention at all check-in points. Bodies lay unburied and dismembered around the harbor, some wearing royal robes and golden signets of the Ancient Bloodline. Crows pecked at their putrid flesh. These Children of Sahael had been dead for at least a day, meaning Natas had taken control of the port before his invasion of the capital had even begun.

Ninti knelt, letting Heziara down from her back and sitting Oadira and Aamira under the cover of the Marula Tree. Ninti glanced over at the tired and confused princesses. There would be no way she could get them to the ships without being captured.

The girls just looked at her, waiting for their next instruction. Images of High Queen Nergal's and Queen Regent Arishkegal's deaths still seemed to reflect in their eyes.

"Princesses of Sahael," Ninti said, clutching the hands of the young girls. "Now is not a time for fear. I need you all to run to that ship over there when I tell you, understand? Split up and get in line. I'll distract the soldiers. Do not hesitate. Do not speak. You are under the protection of your mothers from now until the time you no longer need it. Feel our love and spread it to others as you will."

With the sun rising, fog lifted from the marshes lining the beach.

Now was the moment.

Ninti closed her eyes and exerted her will, using her Hausan powers of Aerokinesis to shift the air currents around her wings. Goosebumps rippled across her skin, tattoos blazing pale gray light. Clouds and mists twirled at her every thought, forming water droplets that descended toward the ground as thick clouds gathered.

The Ennead and Narsan guards shouted and complained as they loaded Sahaelian slaves onto the large sailing vessels.

"Where did this fog come from?" an angry voice cried.

"It's royal witchcraft!" another yelled. "Weapons up! Find whatever noble escaped the purge and cut them down!"

Great Queen Ninti knelt, meeting Heziara at eye level.

"Are you ready, Heziara?" she said to her lovely daughter. The girl cried softly, gray tears falling from her bright eyes. "I wish I could fly us all out of here, but I can't carry everyone. My wings would give out before I got even a hundred feet in the air, and their wind-lances would kill us instantly. Just as High Queen Nergal and Queen Regent Arishkegal, the time for my sacrifice has come."

Ninti used her Hausan artes to conjure a knife, forming air into a solid mass of smooth, clear crystal.

Heziara took the blade from her mother. Her wings drooped, feathers along the edges trembling.

"It's time for you to cut my wrists," Ninti said as she raised her hands. "Just as Oadira and Aamira did for their mothers. Do it now, Heziara! Let my blood seal the spell and protect you until your time of power has come."

Heziara held the knife over her mother's outstretched wrists but hesitated.

"I can't, mama," she pleaded. "I can't."

"You can." Ninti touched Heziara's hand softly and pressed the blade to her own left wrist. Blood spurted as she sliced her primary veins. "Now…the other," Ninti commanded, eyes wide in pain.

With a sob, Heziara pushed the knife into her mother's right wrist. Ninti smiled. Her wings sagged against the Marula Tree as several feathers fell to the dirt. She held her bleeding arms over the bracelet on Heziara's wrist, allowing the blood to flow freely over the jeweled artifact.

"Like my queen sisters,"Ninti breathed,"let my sacrifice seal our bargain. May the Gods watch over and protect you, Daughters of Sahael."

Peace flooded Ninti's body. Her essence entered Nebiriau's bracelet, lighting up Heziara's eyes and royal tattoos momentarily.

Fog swirled around the girls. The ground seemed to shake. For an instant, light danced on their skin and flowed through their veins. And then, like the setting of the sun, the princesses' eyes changed color. Oadira's irises were no longer blue, but dark brown just like other Alkebulan children. Aamira's green eyes no longer shined; the gray of Heziara's deadened and disappeared. Her wings contorted and pulled into her back as if they had never existed.

These were no longer royal princesses of the Sacred

Bloodline. They were average children with average eyes. No glowing tattoos marked their skin, nor wings to set them apart. They were slaves to be sold and to toil away their lives, nothing more. No one would ever know they came from the seed of High Queens and glorious Kings of Sahael.

May the Gods bless them…because no human would.

"Your protection is in place," Ninti said. "Now…I have…one more arte to…perform. Go at my signal."

Weakening, Ninti communicated with the birds in the skies and the Sahaelian forest nearby, commanding the flying creatures to come down and attack the Narsan and Ennead soldiers. Chirps and cries filled the grove as the fowl descended on the troopers. Even long-necked, five-foot tall Kori Bustards, the biggest bird in all Sahael, joined the confusion and tore into their enemies. Dark shapes appeared through the fog as angry soldiers ran in every direction to avoid the onslaught.

"What devilry is this?" someone cried.

"My eyes! It's peckin' my eyes!" another screamed.

Two Kori birds landed in front of the girls. They bowed; crowned heads extending into their black crested chests, while large, three-toed feet dug into the soft soil. Their gray feathers shuttered as they stepped toward the princesses.

"Lead them safely," Ninti whispered as blood pooled on her robes. "They must…make it to the…ships."

Each Kori Bustard took one of the little girls under cover of their large wings and led them away into the fog and confusion of the avian assault. The birds walked quickly, avoiding stampeding soldiers waving their weapons frantically and screaming slavers, until they reached the wooden slats of the boardwalk. The girls kept pace with their feathered protectors. After less than a minute, they reached a line of slaves waiting chained at the gangplank to the largest sailing ship in the water.

The Kori Bustards quickly flew off once the girls were in line. As soon as the birds hit the air, the fog dissipated until the area was clear once again. The dark-skinned Sahaelian slaves looked around knowingly, seemingly unsurprised by the unseasonal and rapid change in the weather.

"What is this?" an old man asked, chains rattling on his wrists as he reached down and touched Oadira's bracelet. His skin was brown and sunken, as if he hadn't eaten in weeks. The girls recoiled, looking around for someone to rescue them. The man smiled kindly though and nodded to several other slaves clad in obsidian fetters next to him.

"Is that…?" a woman asked.

"They survived?"

"Impossible!"

"The Sacred Blood lives!" someone else whispered.

The line of newly enslaved Sahaelians chattered and mingled, until the old man with the gaunt face shushed them all.

"Split them up," he ordered. "Hide the bracelets. Remove their royal garb. Keep them safe."

Several women wearing little more than rags reached over and grabbed Heziara and Aamira, silently hiding them in the crowd of chained people. The old man crouched next to Oadira.

"I'll watch over this young princess for now," he said, smiling bright white teeth. Oadira backed away, wanting to cry out for her mother. "Don't be frightened," the man continued. "I worked in the palace for many years before retiring to the fishing realms here on the coast. I serve the Kings and Queens even now as a humble fisherman. You are safe, young one. The Sacred Blood will live on. We will make sure of it. Sahael has not fallen so long as you and your sister princess breathe."

Back at the Marula tree, Ninti's eyes grew dim. She no longer felt the birds' thoughts or sensed their thrill at soaring the stratosphere. She breathed heavily, waiting for her final breath.

Feet trampled the grass around her. Someone called out, shouting something about a woman with wings bleeding against a tree. Ninti barely paid attention to his words. She was so tired.

Even so, when the dark aura of Lord Commander Natas drew near, Ninti's senses once again became as sharp as polished obsidian.

"Good work," Natas said, voice like a song of deep bass, melodious and beautiful. "I'll take it from here."

He crouched in front of Ninti, dark face shaded by the Marula Tree. His red eyes glowed as he smiled.

"Great Queen Ninti," he said, a playful bounce to his words. "My Narsan and Ennead forces have killed the four kings. I gutted High Queen Nergal. Arishkegal tried to crush my men by collapsing a cave on top of herself. And now here you are, bleeding and dying. What have you done?" He sneered and then asked, "Where are the four princesses?"

"Ek sal jou in die hel sien," Great Queen Ninti responded, spitting in his face.

Without hesitation, Lord Commander Natas unsheathed his onyx sword and stabbed Ninti through the heart. The sword embedded itself in the tree behind her and he let it go, resting as it was in the bark and the queen. He turned to face his two chief officers, General Commander Norg and Commander in Chief Atum of the Ennead Legion.

"Did you find them?" Natas asked. He pulled the sword out of the tree and the woman before wiping the queen's blood from the blade on her own robes.

“No, Lord,” replied General Commander Norg, who looked down from his towering six-foot, ten-inch frame at Ninti’s body. He reached down with his thick arms and picked up the queen’s fresh corpse. Deep crimson blood dripped on his forearm and contrasted against his ebony skin. White teeth shone as General Commander Norg flashed a humorless grin, throwing her body to the ground for the last time. “Those girls couldn’t have gotten far without their mothers.”

“Then they shouldn’t be that hard to find!” Lord Commander Natas yelled, grabbing the guards’ attention. “Pay attention to the princesses’ eyes! They’ll differ from the rest. If one of the queens made it this far, then it’s likely the girls are here. Search every child! Bring them to me! Remove everyone from the ships!”

Natas stomped toward the long lines of obsidian-chained slaves and pointed toward the nearest group. “Start here,” he ordered.

“Understood, Lord Commander Natas!” General Commander Norg said.

Ennead rifled roughly through the crowds of slaves, lining up every little girl under the age of six for inspection.

General Commander Norg started at one end of the line, and Commander in Chief Atum began at the other. They inspected every child, making eye contact with Oadira, Aamira, and Heziara as they went. The commanders placed their hands under the girls’ chins and scrutinized every eye carefully.

Once their work was done, General Commander Norg trudged down the gangplank and walked over to his leader.

“Lord Commander Natas, they aren’t here. We were unable to find them.”

Natas nodded his head and looked to the sky above. “Place

the heads and limbs of the dead into separate piles, their torsos into another," he said, no emotion in his voice. "Do the same to all the dead, disgusting children as well. Send the Narsans into the forest to search for the princesses. We've cleared out Sahaerion, Sahaedeath, Sahaeland, and Sahaedron. They were in none of the capital cities. We must find them at all costs; otherwise, this invasion has been an utter failure."

"Sahael's covered in ash," Norg said. "We've wiped out the Chosen Bloodlines. Those princesses have no home nor family to return to."

Lord Commander Natas looked around, smelling the blood and iron in the air. Sahael's secondary defenses would activate automatically with the death of the queens and kings. He could feel the change in the air. Soon Sahael itself would be an uninhabitable wasteland.

"What's that smell?" one of the Ennead soldiers asked.

Natas picked at his fingernail and cocked his neck to the side with a pop. "Change," he said.

As if in response to the word, the landscape of Sahael began to transmute. The water of the lake lapping a few feet from the tree became cloudy and acidic. Lizards, otters, and birds attempted to escape, but the boiling surfaces quickly consumed all that touched the water.

"What's happening?" a soldier yelled.

"The water is boiling!"

"The land is cursed!"

General Commander Norg walked up to Natas and smiled. "No members of the royal blood remain. The lives of the kings and queens are tied to Sahael's defenses, elements, and the resources of the land."

"As was prophesied, General Commander Norg," Natas said. "Look at the skies. The moment Queen Ninti died, the air grew increasingly toxic. The birds, critters, even the fish are fleeing Sahael with haste." He kicked Ninti's body lightly and turned toward his commander. "We've either enslaved or completely eradicated Sahael's four kingdoms, including Khartoum Palace. Sahael's secondary defenses will exterminate any in hiding."

"Understood," General Commander Norg replied.

"Did you find the princesses?"

"No sir. But if they are here in the land, they will die with the rest."

"Let us hope so." Natas walked back into the Sahaelian forest, eye twitching. The princesses had survived. He knew it. The mission had been a success, and yet still failed…at least temporarily. His revenge would be achieved, of that he had no doubt.

As he trudged past the trees toward the sandy beach, his personal yacht arrived with its red sails and square symbol of the hordes of Natas. Within the hour, the air would be too noxious to breathe. He would not risk a journey on the open ocean while Sahael turned to ash behind him. Norg and Atum could take the yacht and he would meet up with them later. Natas needed time to think. His invasion had failed in its primary objective.

Natas rubbed the onyx ring on his right middle finger, whispering the incantation of Okrelshan. The gemstone glowed brightly as Nebuchadnezzar's portal opened in front of him. Vibrant purples and oranges danced on the surface of the circular gateway. The air tingled with electricity. He stepped through the portal, aggravated with his thoughts. Instantly, Natas arrived back in Naharis's realm, where he would remain until he figured out his next course of action. Failure smelled like brine and vinegar, and right now that was all he could smell.

As ordered, Norg and Atum quickly finished loading the slave ships, boarded the yacht, and sailed Lake Sahael through the river pass while the green forest canopy withered to brown. The other freighters followed, loaded to the gills with Sahaelian citizens to be sold on the outer continents of Aarde. The once great people of Sahael would know what it meant to be weak like everyone else; to be helpless. As far as the slavers and the Ennead legions were conserved, today was a good day.

The Sahaelian people on the other hand were now slaves. Everything they cherished had been ripped from them in a single day. No magic, no army, no vaunted royal family had saved them. One moment they were the most powerful people in Aarde, the next, refugees at best, cattle at worst. They had fallen before they even had a chance to stand.

From the deck of the ships, these exiles watched in horror as their kingdom burned. Smoke filled the Sahaelian air, vegetation withered. Animals from the forests, some as large as Sahaelian bears, jumped into the ocean in an attempt to flee the poisoned land. Waves swallowed them whole and tossed their drowned bodies back on the rocks of the cursed shoreline. Tens of thousands of birds filled the sky above in flocks of every variety. They fled to new lands, never to return.

The young princesses stood at the edge of their ship, the *Nightengale*, terrified, clinging tightly to each other as they watched the Captain, Lynch he was called by his men, make his way across the bow of his ship.

"We've gotta travel through the Sahael River to connect to

its greater lakes and then enter the Middle Passage," Lynch ordered as men rushed to get out of his way as he crossed the deck. "From there, we'll hit the Nautical Pass. Would you look at how fast Sahael is rotting. Natas warned us it would be quick, but by the Gods, you would think the underworld itself was clawing its way up from the depths." He spat over the side and turned back toward his men. "We have about a twelve-week journey ahead of us, so hurry up and pack those vermin in like sardines. There's no time to waste!"

"Aye, aye, Captain," said the crew.

Crammed into the lower decks with their legs secured by obsidian chains, the Sahaelian people were forced to crouch or lie down for some resemblance of comfort. Women and children, the princesses included, were held in separate quarters and, at times, on deck in cages with limited freedom of movement. This exposed them to violence and sexual abuse from the crew. The princesses watched helplessly as many of their fellow captives suffered abuse…but never them. Whenever a sweaty crewman looked their way, it was as if the girls were unappealing, or even invisible.

The Ennead lived on the lowest level, while the Sahaelian slaves occupied levels two, three, and four. The air in the hold was putrid. The heat was relentless and unforgiving as it bore down on them. The lack of sanitation and suffocating circumstances led to a torrent of deadly diseases. Epidemics of fever, dysentery (what the Sahaelians came to call the flux), and smallpox were frequent.

As the *Nightingale* began its journey toward the Middle Passage Gate and Nautical Pass, the concession to endure these conditions swiftly became a reality. Men who had fought back at first found themselves so beaten down, starved, and molested, they would barely raise their eyes when a crew member slapped them.

After several days, Captain Lynch scanned his ship and became increasingly displeased with its filthy conditions. At the peak of his frustration, he slammed his fist onto the *Nightingale's* wooden railing, capturing the attention of his crewmen on deck.

"Get the children! Have them swab this shithole at all five levels," Captain Lynch ordered.

Oadira, Aamira, and Heziara were taken from their cages and placed into separate cleaning groups. Disgusted by their accommodations, the girls retched at the sight and smell of dried human feces, stale urine that had seeped into the crevices of the wood, and the decaying bodies of their fellow brothers and sister.

Given a bucket filled with soiled water, the girls reluctantly got on their hands and knees to scrub the decks. Though their lips remained chapped from thirst and stomachs grumbled due to hunger, the physical pain Oadira, Aamira, and Heziara felt weighed little to nothing compared to watching the crewmen take delight in casting their kin into the sea. Sharks tracking behind the *Nightingale* relished the advantage of such an easy meal.

Once their chores were complete, the princesses were forced back to the lower decks. Luckily, the Sahaelians aboard the ship, especially the women, actively protected the little girls by keeping them clean, clothed, and fed. They had wrapped rags around their bracelets to cover the sacred emblems and would sing them songs of better days behind and hope for better ahead. The enslaved men aided the girls by sacrificing portions of food to ensure they survived the strenuous journey.

After the sixth week of the voyage, the princesses could barely remember their lives from before the ship had set sail. Had they really lived in a palace with kings and queens? Had they really enjoyed so much food that some would go to waste? Had they really watched their mothers dance and sing while practicing magics of arcane potency? It all seemed like a dream wrapped in a waking nightmare of abuse and starvation. Life could never have been that good, because their existence now was so terrible.

One evening Oadira crouched in a corner of the lower deck between two starving women. The ship rocked gently, and she smelled the sea air mixed with the sweat and excrement of hundreds of weak people. She had long since gotten used to the reek. Where Heziara and Aamira were at that moment she didn't know, or care.

Looking to her left, Oadira saw a ten-year-old boy staring at her. She had noticed him before many times as they cleaned the ship or helped move dead bodies up the stairs. Scrawny and sickly, the boy sat with his legs pulled up to his chest. He was barefoot, wearing tattered clothing with dirty dreadlocks. He silently studied Oadira. After several moments, he scooted toward her from the opposite end of the lower deck.

He approached carefully with a warm smile. *"It's okay!"* he said, though no words left his lips. *"My name is Horus. I'm a friend."*

Telepathy! Oadira hadn't heard another person's voice in her head since Queen Ninti died. Immediately, she felt a connection to the boy as he pointed to his beautiful eyes.

The boy pointed to his eyes and for a moment they changed color to a bright blue, just like Oadira used to see in her own irises before she left Sahael.

"Don't be troubled," he said without speaking. *"My people know who you are. Before we arrive at the first port, Captain Lynch will assign five groups of children to stretch their legs and exercise in order to get us ready for purchase. You will be in one of them."*

The young boy smiled while rubbing his cramped legs. His gaze shifted to Oadira's adorned wrists, currently wrapped in scraps of cloth.

"Your bracelet is beautiful," the young boy noted. *"I saw it when you first arrived on the docks with the Kori birds. Don't worry. It will protect you and your sisters. True Sahaelians, Egyptians, and Alkebulans can see you for what you are. I am Egyptian, taught by my parents to be a proud protector of Sahael when I grow up. I will be as strong as my father was. Be brave and stay strong too. We will get through this."*

He walked feebly back to his cage and positioned himself inside. The boy scratched his extended stomach and wiped his runny nose with the sleeve of his tattered shirt.

After what felt like an eternity on the *Nightingale*, Captain Lynch arrived at Upper Louango Port. Stucco and stone buildings rose over the docks; palm trees swaying in the humid breeze.

Oadira was led toward the gangplank with a group of other children.

"Out of the way!" shouted a crewman with missing teeth and scraggly beard.

Behind him stalked two larger sailors carrying a cage that contained the skinny Egyptian boy that had spoken to her using his telepathy.

"This is where we say goodbye until we meet again," he said as he was carried off the ship.

Oadira stood by the railing, out of the way of the crew as they pulled people from the hold and shoved them toward the docks. Heziara and Aamira found their way to her once all the children had been separated from the adult slaves. Watching from the ship, the girls saw the buying and selling of their Sahaelian brethren.

The Egyptian boy's freedom was sold to a tall witan who looked about six feet eight inches tall and dressed in an expensive, medieval tunic with matching trousers and high-quality leggings. He towered over everyone on the pier with a look of regal entitlement. His broad shoulders were draped in a dark-black, hooded cloak. Massive feet rested comfortably in leather boots adorned with solid-gold buckles. As he was presented his purchase, the man's gaze shifted toward the princesses. He walked up the gangplank toward Captain Lynch, who stood near the girls.

"The Madame Lalaurie would like to purchase them," the man said, pointing at the princesses.

"The Madame of Lucedale?" Captain Lynch asked.

"That's correct," said the witan.

"Why?" Captain Lynch inquired. "She's not known to hold interest in slaves so young."

"I'll make it worth your while," the witan asserted. He then handed Captain Lynch a large chest of gold. "I know what she likes, and what she's looking for. These girls will do nicely. They will easily grow into the loveliest women you have in stock here. You're currently on course inside of the Nautical Pass; however, it would be rather beneficial for you to head to the port of Londone instead."

"Why Londone?" asked Captain Lynch, making eye contact with the man. The captain seemed wary, as if the witan wasn't telling him the full truth.

"The Madame's representative will be waiting for your arrival. The representative is in transit from the Aban province. She's aware of your precious cargo of Sahaelian slaves and is willing to pay a hefty price for the best specimens," the witan said calmly, smiling wickedly as his eyes shifted to the princesses.

Captain Lynch eyed the man suspiciously. "How hefty?"

The man sneered. "Let's just say you'll never worry about money for generations."

"What assurances do I have?" asked Captain Lynch, who smiled slightly as if his interest had been piqued.

The man turned and shouted to one of the crewmen. "Hey, you there! Bring up my purchase now!"

The sailor nodded and had one of his colleagues help him lift the cage holding the Egyptian boy. They brought it back onboard and let it drop next to the man with a clang.

"This newly purchased slave boy will stay on the *Nightingale* to make sure those three girls arrive safely and unspoiled," the witan said, tapping his hand against the cage. "Consider this boy my eyes and ears. You are to drop him off in the land of Inheritance when finished, and he will report to me what occurs. If he does not arrive at the land of Inheritance, consider your life, your boat, and your slaves forfeit. This should act as proof of the buyer's sincerity."

Captain Lynch shifted awkwardly. He wanted to know why the three girls were desired, but in his line of work, curiosity was only suited for the foolish. Sticking to his better judgment, Captain Lynch smirked as he shook the witan's hand.

"I'll deliver the boy to the Southern Port of Inheritance in Eastern Aarde and the girls, untainted as promised, to the Port of Londone in Eastern Aarde. Make sure you have my money ready. This isn't a charity, you understand me."

With a cruel grin that could ice over hell itself, the man responded, "Of course. The Madame of Lucedale and I thank you in advance for your patronage."

PART TWO:
THE ORISHAN BLOODLINE

CHAPTER I

A REMEMBRANCE OF SUPPRESSION

Lucedale Colony, June 19, 1500, The Age of Enlightenment

Oadira awoke sweaty and uncomfortable, not from the humid temperatures, but from the images of ships, slaves, white bears, and dead mothers that infected her nightmares.

Fifteen years had passed since the night that forged Oadira's sleeping terrors. She had grown into a mature woman, flawlessly beautiful. She stood six feet five and towered over her captors. She had well-defined muscular legs, an athletic yet slender frame, and braids falling to the small of her back. Her teeth were ivory colored and glistened with perfectly unblemished chestnut skin. Inner strength was more important to her than anything on the surface, yet for some reason she couldn't understand her dreams. In slumber, her body shook uncontrollably as her heart raced. Sweat drenched her linens as terrible memories of her youth filled her subconscious.

Loss, helplessness, and fear plagued Oadira. The thought of being hungry, cold, and in tight, dark spaces without her mother's arms wrapped around her made her claustrophobic and scared. Flashes from dreamscapes reminded her of spilled blood, magic protections, and the three other little girls she hadn't seen for quite some time.

Where were they right now? Did they enjoy a comfortable bed and a peaceful morning as she did, or were they being sold to angry men as wives worth little more than the price of a cow?

She would find out soon enough at the reuniting. Was Oadira excited to see them, or afraid they suffered so much all this time while Oadira lived in a mansion?

A deep breath filled her lungs and forced the remnants of her dream back into the shadows of her mind.

Get it together, Oadira! she said to herself internally.

She rubbed her silky and expensive sheets on her luxurious mattress. She had all the comforts of life: a vanity, a wardrobe, a chest at the end of her bed, a large dresser with twenty drawers, and a table on each side of her mattress with oil lamps. The smell of saltwater and incense permeated the air, making her feel calm and uneasy at the same time.

She heard a knock on the door. It was her maidservant, Amahlé, asking to enter the room, just like every morning.

"Amahlé! Amahlé! You may come in," Oadira yelled.

Amahlé unlocked the door and entered the bedchamber. With warm, light-brown eyes and visible scars all over her neck and ears, the middle-aged woman acted as a mother to Oadira and had cared for her since she arrived at Madame Lalaurie's estate. Amahlé hurried to Oadira and embraced her with open arms.

"Are you all, right?" Amahlé asked, noticing something afflicting Oadira's mind.

"I keep having those dreams," Oadira said.

“Still? Anything new?” Amahlé inquired seeing Oadira’s tense body.

“During my time on the *Nightingale*, I remember being locked in my cage and seeing Nezikiah, a large Alkebulan youth, who was being violated on Captain Lynch’s orders. I don’t recall the reasoning behind it, but witans were surrounding him, initially blocking my view. When a gap between the men opened up, those animals were taking turns inserting themselves inside of Nezikiah until his legs gave out. I could tell they were hurting Nezikiah by his unnatural screams of pain and humiliation. I still hear his screams.”

Amahlé rubbed Oadira’s back softly with her right hand.

“They all laughed,” Oadira continued in a whisper, “imitating his moans and mocking him while having their way within his anus. All I could do was turn away and cover my ears.”

“I’m so sorry you had to deal with that, child,” said Amahlé.

“But that’s not all. This time in my dream, I remembered seeing a sickly Egyptian boy. He watched over me and was also under the captain’s protection. I wonder what happened to him.” Oadira’s questions filled her eyes with tears and self-loathing. “I didn’t even know what happened to my sisters until a few days later. We were separated upon our arrival to our respective hell holes. My sister Aamira was sent to the Vannadale colony, and my sister Heziara was sent to the Abingdale colony.”

Amahlé continued to console Oadira in her arms when she noticed Oadira’s bracelet and rings glowing.

“Oadira,” Amahlé said, hand slowing on her back. “The slaves on the estate look up to you. You bring them joy in a place filled with hatred and despair.”

“Lies!” Oadira shouted, slamming her fist against the bed.

"How can I bring them joy when they remain shackled in magical, obsidian chains? They've been reduced to nothing! Forced to work from sunup 'til sundown. And I've done nothing to alleviate their misery. What joy could I possibly offer? The enslaved males are overworked by the overseers and forced to stand by as their wives, daughters, and sisters are constantly harassed, touched inappropriately, and raped and molested by these evil witans, who look at me and want to dig their claws into me. But they never do! Am I cursed to be safe while I watch those around me suffer?"

Oadira lifted herself from the bed. With her head hung low, she crossed the room and gazed into the mirror.

"The slaves look to you with happiness in their eyes," Amahlé continued, "as if they're forcing the weight of their pain and suffering upon you. If you fail them, they'll lose all hope in their emancipation."

"But how can I emancipate them?" Oadira asked. She was strong, yes, but not like the queens in her dreams. They were regal and powerful…but even they fell before the might of evil.

Amahlé remained hesitant to respond. Instead, she called for the chambermaid to wait on Oadira as she entered her restroom overwhelmed with terrible sadness.

After a few minutes, Oadira finished. The chambermaid grabbed Oadira's pot.

Oadira washed her hands, exited the bathroom, and walked toward the armoire to peruse her wardrobe while Amahlé waited near the door.

After Oadira finished getting dressed, she stepped out from behind her armoire with a lovely, loosely fitted tunic called a cotte with a bliaut over a full chemise with tight sleeves, the pinnacle of fashion throughout the colonies. The beautiful bliaut had a flared skirt with sleeves close to the elbow that widened at the wrist, forming a trumpet shape.

"You look nice," Amahlé said, examining her from head to toe.

Oadira started fidgeting and biting her nails.

"Still anxious?" Amahlé asked, sensing more troubling thoughts weighing heavily on Oadira's mind.

"Amahlé…there's something I need to tell you," Oadira said.

"What's going on, Oadira?" Amahlé asked.

"I'm aware of what happens at the Madame's breeding farms on the estate," Oadira said.

"Is that so?" Amahlé asked. "Does this mean you've been sneaking out again?"

"There is so much more that I can tell you about Madame Lalaurie's breeding farms," Oadira said, avoiding the question. She took Amahlé's hands in hers and squeezed.

"Like what?" Amahlé asked.

"Just this last night, I snuck out through my window and overheard several witan men and women at the breeding farms. I learned that Madame Lalaurie set them up to help produce more slaves for labor throughout the three provinces to help strengthen their economies."

"Did you hear or find out anything else?" Amahlé asked.

"I learned that the boys and the little girls were to be sent to the fields until both were old enough for other jobs," Oadira explained.

Amahlé listened silently.

"The intricate nature of labor on this estate is unstable and unnatural," Oadira said, still holding Amahlé's hands as if the physical connection would somehow help convey the words. "I know they teach the young boys born into slavery how to wrestle at a young age, all for sport and entertainment for witans. They place the little black girls in the kitchen until they come of age to be sold to other brothels to be whores or bed wenches for insecure witans."

Oadira cringed at the thought but continued undeterred.

"I've secretly visited the Madame's breeding farms and spoke with the other slaves. While there, I overheard Madame Lalaurie speaking about your sister and her children. She's sending her to the breeding farms, your nephew to the wrestling camps, and your niece to the kitchens."

Pulling her hands away, Amahlé couldn't hide her look of bewilderment. Her lips moved, but no words left her lips. Though she was well aware of the abuse and inhumanity, it had just never been so blatantly depicted for her by someone so young and beautiful. No one liked talking about any of this, let alone a princess of Sahael. True, the young girl Amahlé waited on was no longer a child. Yet, the lack of emotion in Oadira's voice unsettled her.

Amahlé's shoulders slumped, and her hands started shaking. Oadira quickly grabbed a chair, urging Amahlé to sit down and get her emotions under control for fear of being overheard. Oadira grabbed another chair and sat right next to Amahlé as quickly as she could.

"Don't worry. We'll find a way for your family to escape this estate," Oadira reassured her.

"But how?" Amahlé frantically replied. "If we don't save them as soon as we can, that place will work them to death. Or even worse—send them to the outer lands of Iceoth to be hunted for sport! They'll freeze and be eaten by Mastiffs."

"I have a plan Amahlé," Oadira said quietly.

Amahlé looked at Oadira, hands shaking. "How did you come to have this plan?"

A smile spread Oadira's cheeks, and she glanced at the wooden floor for a second. "Sometimes at night, I pick my room lock to spy on the Madame without drawing any attention to myself, let alone her ire. Other times I climb down my window with a rope ladder that the slaves made for me, giving me the ability to visit with them after they see the candlelight emanating from my window as a signal. I've seen the breeding farms and heard the screams of the women who have their babies taken from them. I've seen and recognized everything on this estate—Madame Lalaurie's deepest secrets, inner workings, and hidden dealings. The Madame speaks so loudly that everyone in the mansion can hear her."

"I see," said Amahlé as she moved her chair to sit behind Oadira. She slowly began removing the blue beads at the end of Oadira's long braids. "Let me fix your hair. It's so beautiful with the slight blue coloring. Let me brush some of it out while I think. Brushing your hair has always calmed me."

After several moments, Amahlé finished removing the rest of the blue beads. Not a word passed between them.

"Are you excited to see your sisters?" Amahlé finally asked, attempting to ease Oadira's mindset by bringing up good news.

"I am excited to see them," Oadira said. Unexpected tears rimmed her eyelids.

Much like Amahlé and the other slaves didn't like talking about the reality of their helplessness, Oadira didn't like thinking about her cousins.

When Oadira, Heziara and Aamira arrived in Londone,

they were separated deliberately per the witan man's instructions. The witan man insisted that the three were to live privileged lives of luxury and comfort. It was one of several conditions Madame Lalaurie and her sisters were given along with the order they would attend the Royal Rumble every year until the girls were 18 years of age. Per the witan man's command, Aamira and Heziara were to live with Madame Lalaurie's two sisters in the colonies of Vannadale, and Abingdale.

It had been several years since she had seen either of them at the Rumble. Neither seemed happy back then, and Oadira always wondered what pains they endured. While Oadira had every comfort, she had no way of knowing whether Heziara and Aamira enjoyed peace or pestilence.

"I wish I could see them more often," Oadira said, quiet tears hitting her upper lip with a saline flavor. "At first, we would meet every year at the Rumble, but now it's rare they arrive at all. I'm glad to have confirmation of their attendance this year."

Although Oadira barely knew them, her connection with Aamira and Heziara was unbreakable. Oadira thought of just seeing them and having a good time once more, just like in the years before.

Madame Lalaurie's voice cut off Oadira's thoughts as it carried from down the hall. She yelled about the floors not being clean enough and shouted to the overseer that she would be traveling for the next few days with Oadira accompanying her.

"Make sure she's healthy and strong as always!" the Madame shouted. "I don't want any blemishes, cuts or bandages. Oadira needs to look her best. We're not going to pay any debts with weak flesh!"

"She's such a caring woman," Oadira hissed.

Amahlé and Oadira sat quietly, listening to Madame

Lalaurie's shouted conversation. The woman's booming voice grew fainter as she walked to another part of the house.

"You're lucky you get to go to the Rumble," Amahlé said, brushing tangles from Oadira's braids. "It sounds very exciting. I've heard the overseers talking about it as they decide what bets they're going to place. Do you know what the participants are wrestling for?"

"Glory, fame, and freedom," Oadira said as the brush tugged on her hair painfully. "If they win, they receive the rights and privileges to procreate with black virgin women of their choosing. It's barbaric. I hope Aamira and Heziara never find themselves as the prize for some sweaty gladiator."

The brush stopped. "Ah, now I understand," Amahlé said. "You're 18 now. Madame Lalaurie wants to pair you and your sisters with a wrestling champion. That's why she has been so worried about what you've been eating and whether you've been sleeping well. I wonder how much money she will make from the deal."

Oadira got up and stared in her mirror with a look of frustration and confusion. Madame Lalaurie, for all her faults, had never hinted this was a possibility. Just last month the woman had mentioned sending Oadira to an embroidery festival for a competition against a madame that had offended Lalaurie. She knew Oadira would win with her skilled needlepoint and wanted to rub the woman's face in it.

Why would she now sell Oadira to a simple wrestler?

"Wait . . . what!?" Oadira asked. "She's just going to discard me like a piece of meat?"

The mirror reflected Amahlé as she stood as well. The scars on her neck and ears seemed more pronounced in the light from the window. "Lalaurie does what she has to in order to survive. She mentioned a debt just now. Perhaps you're the payment…or perhaps you were always meant to be."

Oadira pushed the vanity in complete disgust. It rattled, several perfume bottles falling over and rolling along the surface. She turned and walked over to her window. Warm sunlight hit her ebony skin.

"There has to be a reason for all of this," Oadira whispered. "I'm not going to sit here and wait."

Turning fast, Oadira ran to the door and opened it slowly.

"What are you doing?" Amahlé asked in almost a shouted whisper. "You're not supposed to leave until you're called for."

"If I'm going to be sold off, I want to know for sure." Oadira said before stepping quietly into the hall at the top of the staircase and closing the door behind her. The opulent setting with its carved wooden molding on the walls and white painted banisters had always bothered Oadira, especially when juxtaposed against the quarters enjoyed by the slaves and servants. Still, she had come to enjoy aspects of living here, and didn't want to leave if it wasn't on her own terms.

Madame Lalaurie's voice echoed in the chambers below. Oadira crept down the stairs to the main landing with its polished hardwood floors and tall vases set in alcoves like family heirlooms. The woman continued speaking, occasionally interrupted by the head overseer of the plantation and surrounding factories, Grayven. Lalaurie had a friendly and…intimate partnership with the man, despite his greasy hair and gaunt face.

"Oadira and her sisters are the only eighteen-year-old virgins I have on my family's three estates," Lalaurie said in the next room. Oadira clung to the wall, hoping no one came along to notice her spying.

"I understand that," the head overseer replied in his nasal

voice. “But is now the right time for such a move? These Sahaelians are superstitious. Without the princess here---"

“Every Dalean wrestling trainer will desire three gorgeous virgins to pair with their champion bull,” Madame Lalaurie shouted. “You think our losses are going to evaporate, Grayven? Desperate times, and all that. If a bitch and a bull need to be paired, we may as well reap the rewards now.”

Bitch and bull. The repulsive slurs used to describe black Alkebulan men and women made Oadira’s fists clench.

“Are you sure?” Grayven asked. “Oadira is quite well loved here.”

A brief silence reigned for a moment before Lalaurie answered. Perhaps she too had grown fond of Oadira. Of course, how fond could you really be of a bitch you’re waiting to sell off?

“I’m sure,” Lalaurie stated. “Get the carriage ready. Let’s head to the pens for some…”

A chair scrapped against wood. Lalaurie must be getting up to leave the room.

Oadira darted back up the stairs, hearing the conversation continue into the hall as she made her way back to the room and closed the door behind her.

Amahlé got up from the edge of the bed, face worried. “what happened? Did you hear anything?”

Oadira walked to the window and fell into her armchair. She had no words to convey the powerlessness she felt. Despite what she had told herself for years, Oadira had never mattered in the eyes of Madame Lalaurie; she was just property, not even three-fifths of a person. She knew many witans from the Lucedale colony lusted to deflower her. They had offered Madame Lalaurie substantial amounts of money for the opportunity but were always rejected. Oadira thought this was evidence of the woman’s passing affection for her. But no, Lalaurie simply needed the right motivation and reason to sell her. That motivation apparently came down to desperation. The reason? Greed.

Amahlé smoothed wrinkles from the bedspread, waiting for Oadira to speak.

"I don't know what to say," Oadira whispered eventually. "I have these nice things. Madame Lalaurie takes great care of me."

"Do you really like walking around, looking weak and timid whenever she and other witan women are around to make her feel better—to *fake* how they feel about themselves?" Amahlé asked. Despite her well-trained status as a house slave, Amahlé let anger tinge her words.

Oadira stood, looking out the window on the green fields. Men and women worked in the morning sun picking nuts and berries from one of the thorned brambles. Their scarred hands evidenced their efforts…and their enslavement. The obsidian chains adorning their wrists and waists had a magical effect on the slaves. It subdued them, placing them in a state of melancholy, making them more accessible for the witans to control.

Oadira was a slave too, chained or not. There had never really been any doubt, but at least in her mind she could place a barrier between the thought and the reality.

She could no longer afford to be so naïve.

"When the time is right," Oadira said in a fit of controlled rage. "I will make my escape and leave this place behind without looking back. And then I'll return to liberate all the slaves on this estate."

Floorboards creaked under Amahlé's feet as she walked over and put her arms around Oadira. "You are brave, child. Braver than you know. May your bloodline give you strength in this land of strangers. I will do what I can to help you, but for now, you will have to code switch and play along, looking like the powerless, timid slave girl until the time is right. Do you understand?"

Oadira got up from her chair and paced around the room, thinking to herself about the horrors of what her future may be and how she could escape.

"Continue to be patient," Amahlé said. "And when the time is right, the opportunity will present itself." Amahlé then gave Oadira a kiss on the forehead as she left her room.

The lock clicked behind her. Oadira hated being locked inside her room. She knew Amahlé was only following the Madame's orders of keeping her safe and out of harm's way, but it still infuriated her.

Oadira quickly made her way to the chest at the end of her bed, pulled out a hidden green book, and began reading to distract herself from the overwhelming feeling of forlornness. The practice of reading remained forbidden for all enslaved people on Madame Lalaurie's estate and inside the province. Still, as a privileged member of the household, Oadira had been taught to read, though the only works she was given outside her studies of witan superiority had been smuggled in by other slaves. The books had given her a glimpse of the wider world and taught her to pay attention to the people around her, especially people who thought they were better than her, like Madame Lalaurie and her witan lovers. She observed how they spoke and interacted with one another—how they carried themselves and their mannerisms and ethics. This allowed her to code switch: to act as one of them, even though her skin color was different.

I can't focus right now, Oadira thought, throwing the book back in the chest. She stared at the ceiling in shock, feeling feeble. Every possible scenario of escape ran through her head, along with how she could help Amahlé, and how she could help her people.

After a few hours, a knock echoed from Oadira's door.

Oadira quickly covered the book with sheepskins, bear blankets, and furs before closing the chest once more.

"Who is it?" Oadira asked.

"I am here to walk you to the carriage where the Madame is waiting for you'" the man's voice said. It was Renauld, one of the house guardsmen. "She does not look pleased."

"I'm coming, Renauld" shouted Oadira.

As the door unlocked, Oadira took deep breaths while listening to the pin tumblers in the door click. Her stomach tightened as she waited. As soon as the door opened, Oadira darted through it, sprinted down the hallway, past the servants, and slid down the twisted staircase. She appeared in the center of the foyer, before running through the large double doors, and jumped down the stairs into the carriage without breaking a sweat.

"It took you long enough!" yelled Madame Lalaurie, a much shorter woman than Oadira. The older woman had to look up to meet Oadira's eyes. The Madame's elegantly long, dark-brown, coiffed hair with ringlets didn't match her yellow teeth.

Her cruel expression, developed by years of brutality, erased any beauty that might have been there in her prime.

Oadira settled into the carriage and immediately noticed the paper announcements for the Royal Rumble. Madame Lalaurie had been reading and scanning the announcements with her eyes averted.

As the carriage pulled out of the estate, Oadira could hear the voices of the overseers yelling at the field hands picking cotton, cutting down trees to make wood for homes, ships, and firewood, and slaughtering livestock. Some of the fieldwork became enduring preparation for slaves to be sold and sent back to western Aarde.

"Get back to it, Sahaelian Niggers!" the overseer shouted as he cracked the whip, creating bloody flesh wounds on the slave's backs.

Oadira cringed once more, balling her hands into tight fists around the fabric of her dress. After a moment, she released the cloth, keeping her composure.

The Madame stared intently at Oadira, waiting for a reaction to the shouting, but none came. Oadira was well versed in her role in their performance. She was to endure and not speak. As she rocked from side to side, Oadira stared out the carriage window, eyeing the slew of brothels that dotted the estate. Long lines of wealthy witan men and women stood from dawn to dusk outside those doors, waiting for admittance to fulfill their lusts.

Oadira's stomach knotted. She could only imagine the horrors the enslaved women and men were forced to endure through the nights and days of salacious activities. The thought of men and women being raped and sodomized against their will, all because the witans were consumed with lust toward their exotic bodies, was repugnant to Oadira.

As the carriage moved through the estate, Oadira's gaze became fixated on a sight that caused her a sense of angst, tearing her heart into pieces: heaps of bodies of black women who had died because of extreme exhaustion and malnutrition, or while giving birth or just living in the extreme circumstances of the estate. Their dark-skinned bodies were discarded like sacks of potatoes. Oadira looked at the corpses and remembered the slaves telling her that the dead could sing. Oadira didn't know what it meant, but she certainly wanted to hear their last song.

Or maybe she didn't want to hear it. The sound may have never left her ears again, tormenting her for the rest of her life.

Perhaps the songs were the screams she heard at that moment as they passed next to the birthing house. One shriek pierced the day louder than the others, signaling that a birth was becoming difficult.

Oadira had helped Madame Lalaurie with slave births on many occasions, observing and feeling the anguish on the faces of the birthing mothers. Aarde would not be a forgiving realm to be born into for these slave children.

On one occasion, Madame Lalaurie had shouted to the midwife about the birthing mother, "She is too weak and won't live to make it. Keep her on her right side as I cut her stomach open to pull the baby out." Madame Lalaurie saw the mother as nothing more than a conduit to a new slave.

Oadira's body temperature increased as the screams grew more distant, causing waves of nervous sweat to form across the brow of her forehead and drip down the sides of her cheeks. The salty perspiration burned her eyes. A rush of chills crept down her spine, making her squirm, causing unpleasantness with every beat of her heart as it thumped against her ribcage, triggering hyperventilation.

Oadira knew she needed to get it together quickly, or she would deal with Madame Lalaurie. She took several deep breaths, bringing her body temperature down as the once-nervous, salty sweat cooled her. The wind touched her face through the carriage window.

"Sit up straight, Oadira," Madame Lalaurie said, swatting Oadira in the leg with her hand fan.

She's so repulsive, Oadira thought. She refused to make eye contact with Madame Lalaurie, keeping her face down.

Madame Lalaurie reached over and grabbed the bottom of Oadira's chin. She forcefully turned her head so their eyes met.

"I've been taking care of you for the past fifteen years," the Madame said. "When I tell you to sit up straight, you sit up straight."

"Yes ma'am."

"Good." The madame smoothed out her dress and took a deep breath. "Now, Oadira. As you know, you have come of age. That means it's time for you to make your way in the world."

Make my way as a bull's bitch? Oadira spat soundlessly.

"That time is today." Lalaurie continued. "It is time for you to help this estate financially. As you know, I've never required you to work the fields. I've protected you as if you were my own daughter. Now you will repay me for my kindness. At tonight's event, the Royal Rumble winner will impregnate you."

The Madame continued looking directly at Oadira. Was it jealousy Oadira saw in the woman's eyes as she looked her over, starting with her long, muscular legs, her thighs, stomach, chest, and then resting on her face? How the madame must hate people more beautiful than her.

"I have made several arrangements with the event owner for breeding rights," Madame Lalaurie said.

Oadira refused to break eye contact. Her eyes became tighter slits with each word Lalaurie spoke.

Suddenly, the Madame smacked Oadira, pointing her finger. "Know your place, Nigger bitch. You want to look me in the eye, you do it with some goddamn humility for my grace and kindness toward you. I could have put you out with the whores if I'd wanted. But you and your sisters were purchased as investments. If it weren't for Vizier Nakhtpaatan, we would have never come to the docks to find you and your sisters."

Oadira's cheek stung from the slap, but she held firm and quiet. One day Madame Lalaurie and all those like her would feel the sting of their own hubris.

"Madame Lalaurie, we have arrived," the carriage driver said, interrupting their uncomfortable conversation.

The carriage driver got out and opened Madame Lalaurie's door, allowing her to exit. Oadira followed as they stepped onto the stone tiles leading to the docks. The air smelled of saltwater while gulls squawked overhead.

"This way, Madame Lalaurie." The carriage driver swept his hand in the direction of the Narsan guards standing at attention in front of the gangplank toward the ship that would take them to the nearby port of Aloe.

Narsan guards.

Behind them stood a group of soldiers Oadira recognized as members of the Ennead Legion, by the decorative patterns in their obsidian armor. Cloaks infused with Orichalcum, a rare metal harvested in Sahael, shined in the sunlight. Their ebony blades, axes, and long swords were also made with the valuable and magical steel, encrusted with onyx and gold.

Oadira's heart began to pound against her rib cage; her hands suddenly became sticky. She had not seen Narsan and Ennead guards outside pictures in her history books since she was a child. Memories of running through a forest flashed in her mind, along with the feeling of holding onto white bear fur as wind buffeted her face.

"Madame," the lead guard bowed. "Allow us to escort you and your slave onto our vessel for the brief voyage."

"And who's ship is that, soldier?" Madame Lalaurie asked, pointing to a large yacht much bigger than their own vessel, with red sails and the square symbol of the four L's symbolizing Narsa. "It's casting a shadow on our ship. I do hope it's someone important that is gracing us with their presence."

"It is, Madame," the guard said, head tilting toward the ship. "That is Lord Commander Natas's personal command vessel."

Oadira almost threw up.

Natas.

She suddenly saw red eyes in her mind, with a dark and angry face plunging a blade into Queen Ninti's chest. She smelled the water of Sahael as it became rancid and putrid while Natas stood on the beach next to the Marula tree yelling for his soldiers to find her and her cousins, the sisters of her childhood.

Natas had been gone. He was a nightmare of the past. There must be some mistake.

Madame Lalaurie's face seemed to confirm Oadira's fear. The woman's skin suddenly drained of color as if someone had pulled a drain plug.

"Lord Commander Natas is here?" she asked, voice cracking slightly.

"Yes, my lady," the guard said as he turned from the gangplank of their ship toward the towering yacht. "In fact, I have been ordered to invite you to join Lord Commander Natas for the voyage. I don't need to remind you what an honor such an invitation is."

Keep it together, Oadira said to herself. The thought of seeing Natas, the man who was whispered about by the slaves and plantation owners alike with fear and trembling, made her knees quake. You would have thought he was the devil himself, and perhaps he was. The stories the children and old women told about Natas were just that to them: stories. Oadira had seen his face as the slaves had led her and her cousins onto the ships that long-ago day. She had run from his rage. She had cut the throat of her own mother with the assurance she would be made safe. Though the memories were faint, and she had done her best to oppress them, they all flooded back at the thought of seeing Natas in the flesh.

"Well…of course," Madame Lalaurie stammered as they stepped into the shadow of his ship. "We would be…" she swallowed, "honored to join Lord Commander Natas on the voyage. It has been some years since I've heard of his presence in the Londone area."

As they approached the gangplank, flanked by even more soldiers, Oadira worried she would faint.

What's happening to me? Keep walking. Keep walking.

He had been hunting her, Heziara and Aamira, right? That's what she remembered the queens saying. Was he still hunting them? Would he recognize her? Was she in danger? The worries of being married off to some wrestler suddenly became infinitesimally small in the face of seeing Natas again.

They boarded the yacht, stepping onto the deck with its polished black wood and smells of moist canvas. Boots thumped loudly against the deck as a large man approached, taller than Oadira; taller than everyone. His dark-skinned face was framed by dreadlocks that hung down to his chest, covering the red and black armor adorning his torso and shoulders.

"Welcome," Natas said, leaning down and kissing Madame Lalaurie's hand. His voice was deep and beautiful, like a lie you tell yourself in the dark of the night. "I am pleased you could join us. I am told you will be presenting some virgins to our bulls at the Rumble. What a blessing for our warriors. I would invite you to leave your slave below deck while you join us for lunch."

"I would be honored, Lord Natas," the madame said with a quivering smile.

Hands shaking almost uncontrollably, Oadira knew she had to keep her composure, or she'd be killed right away. He didn't seem to recognize anything about her.

Her finger and wrist felt suddenly warm. Njiru's rings and Nebiriau's bracelet glowed a pale blue, apparently reacting to Natas's presence, and warning Oadira of danger. She put her hands behind her back quickly and bowed her head to avoid eye contact with the beast of a man.

"Your hair color is unique, daughter," Natas said. He reached up to one of Oadira's braids and touched the pale azure tresses. "Few Sahaelians enjoy such shades naturally." He paused and looked into her eyes. "A pity your eyes do not match."

Natas dropped the hair and turned to speak with one of his crewmen.

Oadira shook inwardly. It required all her strength to keep on her feet. He had touched her hair, searched her eyes, called her 'daughter.'

She hated him.

He was a demon from hell as far as Oadira was concerned.

After a brief discussion with his Bozeman, Natas turned toward the gathering. "Welcome aboard. Those of you who are servants, your quarters are below deck. You will serve, as is your station, doing whatever you are ordered to do. Now, I invite my honored guests to join me for a meal."

Madame Lalaurie turned, face pale. She quickly ordered Oadira, her other servants and carriage drivers, to join Lord Commander Natas's albino maidservants.

"Clean up after everyone throughout the night, and once the dinner party and entertainment has concluded," Lord Commander Natas ordered his staff. "Make sure everyone is locked below so as to avoid any unpleasantness." He smiled, but he may as well have been scowling.

Seeing Oadira's expression, Madame Lalaurie asked to be alone with her for a few minutes. Natas nodded and walked toward a large cabin area where music played, and other guests milled about laughing.

"You heard the Lord Commander," Lalaurie said, glancing over her shoulder as if she were as uncomfortable as Oadira. "You will be with the servants. You've never done this before but follow their lead. Stay away from the others. Don't draw attention to yourself. Don't go near the crew members. I can't have anyone…harming you. You will be seeing your cousins Aamira and Heziara for the last time once we arrive in Aban. I suggest that you enjoy your time together." Lalaurie took a step back as if to leave but paused. "I will…miss you, Oadira. Your presence has never been a…burden to me."

Oadira scoffed inwardly. In her own way, Madame Lalaurie had at least some affection for Oadira, but it seemed like the same affection an owner has for their dog, or a pet they can no longer afford. Even so, when she heard those words out of the Madame's mouth, Oadira knew she had to act as if she too cared that she was leaving the kennel.

"I feel the same way, Mother," Oadira said, using the term she knew would most endear her to the Madame. The Madame turned to walk away, but Oadira realized for the first time she would not be returning to the plantation. What about the people she cared about? Without thinking, Oadira reached over and grabbed Lalaurie's arm just above the elbow. "Madame Lalaurie, wait! What is going to happen to Amahlé and her family?"

The woman turned and glanced down at the brown fingers clenching her creamy skin. Her forehead compressed, pinching her nose. "Don't ever touch my witan skin again," Madame Lalaurie said.

Oadira slowly removed her hand from the Madame's arm.

If I could slap this witan bitch, I would, Oadira said internally.

"Amahlé and her spawn are none of your concern! I'll do as I please with her…with all of them," Madame Lalaurie spat.

"But Madame," Oadira said.

"Mind your business, child!" Madame Lalaurie said.

Two witan women appeared, approaching out of the corner of Oadira's eyes. They were dressed like Madame Lalaurie with similar features and body types, though one was heavily overweight. Oadira turned her head in their direction as they approached. She recognized them instantly.

Martha and Delphine Lalaurie. The madame's ugly and selfish sisters.

"There you are," Martha said, dirty-blonde hair perfectly curled and hanging down in front of her brown eyes. She was five feet six-inches tall. Martha visited from the Vannadale colony. Delphine, the middle sister, had brown hair, brown eyes, and a pudgy frame. She was the same height as Madame Lalaurie and as round as she was tall. Delphine visited from the Abingdale colony.

The two of them were just like their older sister. The only difference was they were quiet about their evilness. Oadira listened as they whispered to each other, oblivious of her presence. They needed to discuss and work out how much money they would need to clear the rest of the Madame's debts with the Lucedale government. They needed to get it taken care of as soon as possible. If they failed, other slaves would need to be sold to another estate to help the Madame clear some of her debts.

"Hopefully this tall one here will bring in enough," Delphine said with a nod of her head toward Oadira. "You've gotten us into a real mess, sister dear."

"Shut up," Madame Lalaurie hissed. Delphine stared daggers at the Madame and placed her hands on her hips accusingly. “We were all blackmailed together, Delphine. Don’t you forget it.”

They continued bickering about how they all were now in debt because of the extra-legal expenses of Madame Lalaurie after she killed her maidservant and late husband fifteen years ago to gain her fortune.

Oadira actually remembered what had happened. She had only been at the plantation for a few months, but she was tasked to clean up the mess after the master’s head had been smashed in with a statue from the mantle. The Madame was too intoxicated to do or remember anything, and both sisters, who had been visiting at the time, were inattentive, clueless, and ditzy. Martha had blacked out too due to too much alcohol. That left Oadira and Delphine to clean up the pieces to save everyone from jail and execution.

What a family they were, blathering and swearing like hens pecking at each other.

Oadira could see the look of frustration on Madame Lalaurie’s face, and in that moment it all made sense. The three sisters needed to clear a substantial amount of debt to ensure that their estates and the slaves were all paid for in full. Someone was blackmailing them regarding the murder, and they had mortgaged everything to pay them off. Oadira and the other two prized virgins would be the price for them to keep their lifestyle and their titles.

“Make sure the other girls are at the Rumble on-time, sisters,” the madame said, face angry and flushed. “I have to go mingle and eat some lunch with men like Natas.”

“Don’t embarrass us,” Martha sneered. “You’ve heard the stories of what Natas---”

“Shut up and be on time!” Madame Lalaurie yelled. “We have a few days, is all. You better have those girls at the Rumble as promised.” She turned toward the sound of music and stalked off.

Once the Madame was gone, her two sisters stared at Oadira hatefully. Martha slowly walked up to her and stopped mere inches in front of her face. Before she could spew her venom, Delphine grabbed her baby sister's arm.

"No need to berate the girl tonight," Delphine said. She reached across and caressed Oadira's cheek with the back of her hand. "She's going to pad our purse tomorrow. Such beauty is bound to fade, my dear. When it does, even the lowest slave lover will not want you as a bed wench."

Delphine turned and walked away. Martha snickered like a schoolgirl, following closely behind.

Oadira turned her back to the two women, hiding her smile at the apparent jealousy the witan women harbored for her. She walked away quietly and confidently, filled with a satisfaction that she had never experienced until now.

They would have no money from her sale. She would escape that very night if needed.

No. She would see Heziara and Aamira again. They could all escape together.

Oadira followed the other slaves and servants to the lower decks, reading the signs leading to the hold at the bottom of the yacht. She acted as if she couldn't read, asking others where to go from there. One of the ship's servants pointed her in the right direction.

The servants escorted Oadira to her sleeping quarters below the ship's main deck. They resembled those of her bedroom back at the Madame's estate. The albino guide left her to herself and made her way back to the yacht's top deck, locking the door behind her.

Oadira was now in a familiar position once again.

But it would only be temporary.

And it would be for the last time.

CHAPTER II

BLOODLINE SECRETS

Aban Province

At sunrise, the yacht arrived in the port of Aloe, where an entourage of servants and Narsan soldiers waited. Oadira continued to look at them with hatred.

Stay in control of your thoughts, she would whisper to herself. *Act the slave. Don't question. Smile through the pain.*

And she did smile.

Oadira was requested to be at Madame Lalaurie's side, among the group of wealthy witans who wanted to tour the city. The group walked along the busy cobblestone streets, passing by many Sahaelian slaves connected by obsidian chains latched around their necks, torsos, and ankles. They all made eye contact with Oadira. The men, women, and even children noticed Nebiriau's bracelets and Njiru's rings immediately, understanding what they represented from the stories still being passed down after 15 years of torment.

As the group passed a food vendor selling roasted chickens and pork legs, Oadira wondered about Amahlé. Deep down, she knew Amahlé was going to the breeding farms or one of the Madame's laboratories for experimentation. If she went to the laboratories, the Madame would mutilate her, severing her limbs to find out how much pain she could endure before death. These experiments had taught the witans just how far they could push their punishments.

The hustle and bustle of people heading in every direction, the loud overlapping conversations, the shouting auctioneers, and the rattling of the obsidian chains gave Oadira violent flashbacks to her time on the slave ships. She observed a group of runaway slaves who had been punished in front of a crowd on an execution block. Their necks, torsos, or ankles were free of their chains, but the executioners had cut off the toes of one man, a woman's left breast, the ears of several children, and the genitalia of several men as punishment for trying to escape. This was not the first time Oadira saw slavery in action. It enraged her and disgusted her. Her breathing increased rapidly; she knew she had to get it under control quickly.

Code switch, code switch, code switch, she told herself.

Her shortness of breath made her almost stumble and fall to the ground, but she quickly regained her bearings. She took a deep breath to gather herself and her thoughts of unleashing her wrath against the witans who found it completely acceptable to keep her Sahaelian brothers and sisters in chains. That a group of people were considered inferior to another based on the color of their skin didn't make logical sense to her. She knew some of it had to do with resentment as well. After all, Sahael had ruled over all for centuries. Now those who wanted power for themselves had achieved their goals, but where Sahael had promoted peace and unity, the other nations cared only for their own comforts.

The group continued to move through the cobblestone streets, desensitized to everything around them. After a short, ten-minute walk, they arrived in Aban City, ready to board Captain Lynch's slave ship, the *Nightingale.* Natas's yacht was not equipped to handle the rough channel waters of the ocean pass.

It seemed everything about this trip to the Rumble was meant to reopen mental scars in Oadira's mind. Either that, or Madame Lalaurie had chosen the *Nightingale* on purpose simply to once again display her power over the taller woman.

The massive ship, though remodeled and cleaned from top to bottom, still bore the scent of dead slaves—their bones, feces, and blood. The ship still carried the obsidian chain hooks that kept slaves from sitting down and resting. A queasy and light-headed feeling came over Oadira as she walked across the deck where she had lied awake at night on more than one occasion, shivering in her cage with the other children. Unable to hold back the revulsion any longer, Oadira rushed to the railing and vomited over the side.

The Madame and her sisters just looked at her with their arms folded in disgust, tapping their feet against the wood in embarrassment.

"For the sake of the Gods," Martha cursed. "We've been on the ship for 30 seconds and she's already seasick? These Sahaelians are certainly weak stomached. Once I was watching one of our bitches be whipped and she peed herself right there. Like a dog. Can you imagine? Filthy creatures."

Oadira slumped to the deck, spitting over the side as she slipped.

Keep it together, Oadira yelled at herself.

"Hurry. Oadira!" Madame Lalaurie said. "Everyone is boarding the ship behind us. Get up! You have done enough to embarrass me,"

Oadira wiped the sides of her mouth and stood; doubt creeping into her mind with each step she took.

Concentrate, focus, and breathe.

Captain Lynch, looking far statelier and more official than he ever did back in his slaving days, sailed down the Aloe private river for several days until they arrived at their intended destination. Oadira had hoped Heziara and Aamira would be brought onboard at some point during the journey, but so far, no other ships had rendezvoused with them.

The quartermaster ordered Oadira, the slaves, and the servants to clean the deck as the distant shoreline and gleaming city drew closer. While cleaning, she overheard one servant whispering to the others.

"*Dit is Kiziah se tyd,*" the older woman said.

Oadira heard the others talking about her as well, their eyes lingered but avoided direct contact. They continued saying to themselves, "*Dit is Kiziah se tyd.*"

Why would they say this? Oadira thought. *What does it mean?* She remembered so little of the old language. She hadn't heard it spoken regularly since Sahael was invaded.

After more scrubbing on her hands and knees, she began to remember a few of the vowels the kings and queens would use when she was little.

'Dit is Kiziah se tyd.' Kiziah was a name. The rest? Something about time. 'It is Kiziah's time?' That seemed right.

"What do you mean, 'it is Kiziah's time'?" Oadira asked one of the slave girls as she sloshed a bucket of soapy water onto the deck.

The girl shook her head and didn't answer. No one seemed eager to talk to her, though their eyes constantly wandered in her direction. Oadira had become used to this sort of thing at the plantation where she was known, and the stories of Sahael were told regularly, but here among strangers, it was disconcerting to have so much attention. She listened to the slaves' conversations as best she could, eavesdropping like she had learned at the Madame's estate. Her hearing had always been excellent, to the point that Madame Lalaurie had taken to having her personal conversations as far from Oadira as possible.

A few of the servant girls about Oadira's age wiped the battlements nearby, complaining about how much Madame Delphine relished the chance to beat any Sahaelian slave; man, woman or child. She listened as they whispered about Oadira specifically and the other two princesses who had been lucky so far not to have to work in the fields or be raped by drunk men to pay their mistresses debts, but that soon the princess' luck would run out.

"They're weak," one of the girls spat. "Did you see how the one threw up when she walked on the ship as if she'd never smelled shit before? They deserve what they're going to get."

"And what do we deserve?" Oadira asked, still kneeling on the deck with a brush in her hand. The girls looked startled that she had overheard them. "No," Oadira continued, voice strong. "Keep talking. Tell me what I deserve. Do I deserve to be raped? Do you?" She returned to her scrubbing. "Perhaps that's the difference between you and me. I don't believe anyone deserves pain."

"You're spoiled and pampered," one of the girls said with a dismissive wave.

Oadira wanted to run over there and pitch the girl overboard but caught sight of Madame Martha stepping onto the deck at that moment.

Code switch. Don't let them know your thoughts.

"Madame Lalaurie has taken great care of me for the past fifteen years," Oadira said more loudly. Madame Martha stopped and began paying attention to the conversation. "The Madame loves me like her own daughter," she continued. "She would allow no harm to come to me. She has gone to great lengths to protect me. And she will continue to go to great lengths to protect me,"

The servants looked at Oadira incredulously. Madame snapped her fingers and barked for the women to get back to work. As she passed, Martha slapped one of the servant girls.

Oadira cringed inwardly. The girl was naïve and stupid, every bit as naïve and stupid as Oadira pretended to be. What Oadira deserved was up for debate, but she knew in her heart that no one deserved to be slapped like that.

As if in response to her musing, the enchanted bracelet and Njiru's two rings began to glow again, lightly, but noticeably. They would sometimes glow when Oadira awoke from her nightmares, but rarely in other circumstances. They seemed to be lighting up with more frequency since leaving the plantation, a fact that frightened Oadira. If the bracelets drew the attention of the Madame, or some greedy slaver, or the Gods forbid, Natas himself, death would certainly follow.

Oadira remained calm, controlling her emotions, and biting her tongue. The rings and bracelet returned to their ordinary, non-magical state.

Keep it together; we can get through this. Then as if spoken by someone else, words came to her mind, and she whispered them out loud. "I know what I am. I am the last of my bloodline, the Orishan bloodline."

A warmth filled her chest. Whatever the words meant, she knew they were true.

After cleaning the deck, Oadira was ordered to scrub the vessel's bottom. Eager to put space between her and the Madame's sisters, she hastily obeyed. As she walked in the direction of her newly assigned task, she noticed some girls eyeing Nebiriau's bracelet and Njiru's rings. They bowed as she entered.

After several more hours of cleaning, Oadira sat in the corner and rested for a few minutes. Her arms ached. She had worked in the plantation mansion for long hours before, but nothing quite as grueling as this. Perhaps she was a bit more pampered than she cared to admit.

One of the older servants came over and sat next to Oadire. Her ears had been cut off at some time in the past, and the woman rubbed them continuously. She fidgeted as if unable to get comfortable.

"You look tired," the woman said.

Oadira nodded. She didn't feel like talking.

"You are one of the virgins," the woman continued. "I recognize the bracelet on your wrist and the rings on your fingers. Most see them as baubles given to you by your mistress, but I see them for what they really are. Many of us do. I am Kiziah."

Kiziah. The name the other servants had been whispering.

"I heard some of the servants say your name," Oadira admitted.

"Yes," Kiziah nodded. "I am a keeper of the old tales. I know much that has been forgotten in just a handful of years. Oppression will do that. Few of our people remember the power and wealth we enjoyed, even though it was less than a generation ago. I sense your pain, daughter of Sahael."

Oadira dropped the brush and covered her eyes with her hands, suddenly overcome and overwhelmed with a tremendous amount of emotion, pain, and stress. It was as if Kiziah was giving her permission to feel all of it.

"Let it out," Kiziah said with a soft shushing sound. "You carry a burden you don't fully understand. You and the other princesses. Don't fret. The Gods have their eyes on you."

At the sound of approaching footsteps, Kiziah's voice fell silent. They all rushed back to their working positions.

An overweight witan descended the steps and stopped just before he reached the bottom. He pointed his stubby index finger at Oadira, making eye contact with her. Oadira avoided his gaze.

"You," the man barked, licking his lips. "You're ordered to come with me."

Oadira continued to ignore him, scrubbing the floor with her tired arms.

"Oi!" the man shouted. "I just gave you an order, slave!"

Before the man could step closer, a bell rang on the top deck, signaling the time for Oadira and the others to return to their quarters per Madame Lalaurie's instruction. Oadira got up from her duties slowly with pain in her arms, wrists, and back and a lot of sweat dripping down her face. She passed the man, who stood at least a foot shorter than her, and stomped up the stairs. Oadira entered her quarters and prepared for bed.

A mirror hung in the corner, a luxury as far as any of the other slaves would be concerned. Oadira examined her beauty, physique, rings, and bracelet, lit brightly by the bracelet's sapphire glow.

Why were the bracelet and rings glowing so often? How could she keep them from doing that?

As if in response to her question, the jewelry blazed brighter than before, seemingly filling the room with their light. Oadira's eyes transformed in that instant, mimicking the sapphire color pulsating from her rings and bracelet. She blinked slowly, staring at the blue pupils that seconds before had been a pedestrian brown.

Words rang in her mind with such potency she needed to say them out loud.

"What is my purpose?" she said. "I know what I am. I am the last of my bloodline, the Orishan bloodline."

A feeling of pain washed over her; not her pain, but the pain of the women around her. She could feel their fear and anguish. How much they suffered.

She finally released her breath.

What was that? she asked herself. An overwhelming urge filled her body. She wanted to be with her people. She wanted to see their faces and share in their pain.

The glowing bracelet and rings quickly faded once more, as did the color of her eyes. Instead of blue, they were brown once more.

Oadira opened the door leading to the ship's side and watched as a group of slave girls entered the custodial rooms. She could see the anguish and pain on their faces and the trauma on their bruised bodies with every step they took. Whatever pain and fatigue Oadira felt from the day's labors, theirs was greater.

Oadira followed them and entered the custodial area where they were staying. None of them had their own room like Oadira. She watched them move bales of hay to create makeshift beds, preparing to sleep with the rats and cockroaches. Her heart ached for them.

"Do you girls want to stay somewhere clean where you can wash up?" she asked. "I have a room. The bed can probably sleep nine people, it's so big."

They all replied 'yes' and were very grateful that they would have a nice place to sleep for the next several days. They grabbed their belongings and followed Oadira back to her quarters. The girls washed themselves of their sweat, and perhaps the stench of witan men who had forced themselves on the girls during the voyage.

They all settled in for the night and relaxed among each other, taking whatever space was available in the clean bed. Oadira could feel the pain and trauma in their bodies as they tried to sleep, knowing all the sexual violations they had endured, doing so many things against their will. Oadira wanted to do something about it; she wanted to exit her room and choke the life out of the fat witan who had tried to order her to sleep with him, and those who saw nothing wrong with people like her in chains.

How much longer must my people suffer at the hands of our oppressors? she asked herself while lying on the floor in the dark, hearing the breathing of her slave sisters all around her. Let them have the bed. Many of them may never have slept comfortably before. Oadira could spend the night on the floor for once.

"One day, we will all rise, take up arms, and kill every witan that has slaves or shares the same prejudices," Oadira whispered as she looked over her people.

After a few minutes of silence, a knock echoed through the room.

"Who is it?" Oadira asked quietly.

"Kiziah, my princess."

Oadira stepped lightly to make sure she didn't disturb any of the sleeping girls, lit the oil lamp, and opened the door. Kiziah stood there, rubbing her severed ears.

"May I speak with you, princess?"

"I'm not a princess," Oadira said.

"Surely others have called you 'princess' before."

"A princess doesn't live as a slave in a plantation house. A princess doesn't clean the deck of a ship. A princess doesn't thank the Gods she didn't have to fight off a fat witan to keep her virtue."

"But you are a princess, as everyone has told you your entire life." A look of compassion filled Kiziah's face. "You are more than you know. May I enter so we can talk?"

"Of course. Come in. Careful to be quiet. These girls are tired and fell asleep almost immediately."

"This is the only peace they know in life," Kiziah said as they entered the room, "It is kind of you to let the girls sleep in the bed. They look cramped, but I'm sure none of them will complain." She leaned over and caressed the head of one of the girls lying near her, dark hair glistening in the lamp light. "This one is named Kanji. She is strong. I sent her to please the man who ordered you to go with him."

Odira stepped back. "What do you mean, 'sent her to please him?'"

"I feel Nergal speaking to me, child," Kiziah said. "She is prompting me to help save you on this final leg of your journey."

"But…" Oadira stuttered. "I don't want anyone else suffering for me."

"It isn't your choice," Kiziah said. "I know the tales of Sahael and the ancient bloodlines because I was there. I served the kings and queens in Khartoum Palace. I know of the powers of our people. You have been protected by that bracelet and those rings. You think that protection meant others didn't have to sacrifice in your stead? Of course, they did. Tonight was just another example of that protection, where someone else took your place."

Oadira wanted to cry and throw up and scream and murder all at once. She knew Madame Lalaurie had placed her in multiple situations where she might lose her virtue, intervening to make it look as if she had saved Oadira. It was all planned so that she would have a particular type of dependence on the Madame.

Someone else was always chosen to suffer so Oadira didn't have to. At first, she thought it was a blessing. Now she realized it was a curse.

"They were always looking for ways to get themselves out of their situation," Oadira said, sitting on the floor with her arms clenched tightly around her legs, while the other girls slept in her king-sized feather bed. "All the women I've ever known. They just wanted out. I want out, and I've never suffered the way they've suffered."

Kiziah sat beside her and wrapped her arm around Oadira's shoulders. "Are you alright?"

Oadira laid her head on Kiziah's shoulder, feeling her comfort and love. "I live in constant fear. I fear for my life every day. I fear that without my virtue intact, I am worthless to the Madame. And here are women and girls slated for the sex farms, at the mercy of witans for their exotic pleasures. All at the expense of the Lalaurie family."

Oadira could see Kiziah focusing on her bracelet and her rings.

"You feel deeply, don't you, Oadira?"

"I suppose."

"You understand the power of those bracelets?"

"They glow," Oadira replied. "Sometimes I feel things I shouldn't be able to feel. Just tonight, I thought my eyes glowed along with the bracelets and I felt the pain of these women."

Kiziah nodded. "The stories of Sahael aren't stories. They're history. We are a rich and proud people, powerful beyond reason. Many of the people in Aban City know of the signs as I do. The symbols on your bracelet tell of the royal family. When people see them, they will be given hope. Hope is a powerful thing, especially for people who have none. These rings and bracelet allow you the ability to feel and experience the worst of what every woman feels. You can jump into and out of the feelings of others briefly for a short time to understand them."

"I don't want to feel those things," Oadira whispered. "That's too much for anyone to bear."

"But you must bear it," Kiziah said. "You have been bearing it without realizing. Think about it. Tell me about a time when you felt the pain of others."

Silence filled the room. Even the breathing of the sleeping girls had stopped, as if they all held their breath.

"I remember coming upon a locked door I had to force open," Oadira began. "I had heard something inside…felt something. Once inside, I remained hidden and observed several female slaves being experimented on for anatomical research. They did it to advance their knowledge of the female reproductive system to find out a way to prevent pregnancies among the Sahaelian, Egyptian, Hornan, and Alkebulan bloodlines. I later found out they wanted to exterminate and eliminate the populations for Natas." Oadira closed her eyes, tears streaming down her face. "The women were in so much pain," she sobbed. "I could feel it. I felt every cut, every moment of fear. I lay hidden, unable to move. Eventually I felt their deaths."

Kiziah held her close as Oadira wept. "Shhh, child. It's alright. You're beginning to understand yourself and your role in all of this."

"Lord Commander Natas was here on his yacht," Oadira said between sobs. "He was here, and I was so afraid when I saw him. I was as afraid as those women had been that night. I thought I would die. For weeks, months, years, I would awaken from nightmares, drenched in sweat from everything that I remembered." Oadira reached for the bedspread hanging off the edge next to her and wiped her nose.

"Is anyone aware of the bracelet's power?" Kiziah asked. "Has anyone seen it glow before?"

"They've only started glowing more recently," Oadira said. "One night when I snuck out of my room, I walked around the estate, pretending I was free. I heard the Madame's overseers saying they saw blue light coming from my window as I slept. Madame Lalaurie didn't believe them but started staring me in the eyes after that, like she was angry and afraid of me. Rumors spread across the colonies, and slaves started looking at me more closely."

"What do you remember of Sahael and the invasion?" Kiziah asked.

"Not much. I have flashes of memory, usually in my nightmares. I remember my mother and father only a little. I remember the fear of that day, and the smell as the land started to die as we sailed away. None of it seems real. I've heard the Madame and her servants talk about a search occurring for four baby girls with eyes the colors of sapphire, emerald, hematite, and turquoise," Oadira continued. "The Madame said they would be in a group of four and that they were inseparable. After the incident with the blue glow in my room, she ordered her overseers to spy on me, and that if it were to happen again, they were to alert her at once. Luckily, Amahlé, my caretaker who raised me, helped me cover up any mistakes and keep me protected as a new teenager. Even then people would whisper that me and the other girls had been found in a trio, not in a group of four, and so we couldn't be them. And our eyes were normal, so that was it."

Kiziah squeezed Oadira's hand. "You are not normal, Daughter of Sahael. We all know that."

"Sahael isn't real. It's a fantasy we tell ourselves to pretend we've ever been anything more than slaves.

"We are more," Kiziah smiled. "Even in our pain, we are more. And remember, young Oasira, some of us remember Sahael to this day. Even you, so young, have memories of that sacred place. Don't deny it, Princess. We look to you now for freedom and salvation; for a return to The Motherland of Alkebulan."

Oadira looked up to see all the young women who had been sleeping in her bed were now leaning over the edge looking at her and Kiziah. The soft light from the lamp danced in their eyes.

"What can we do to help you, Princess of Sahael?" one of them asked.

Oadira felt a swelling of love in that instant. These women had no hope, and yet now they looked to her as if Oadira had the power to overthrow the nations with the power of some ancient bloodline.

"Just be ready for now," she smiled, not sure of what else to say. "We move along through our everyday activities and not bring any negative attention to us. Since setting out from my plantation, I've been plotting my escape. When the time is right, I will act. I invite all of you to join me. Be ready."

Again, Oadira wiped the tears away from her face with her cotton bedspread.

The girls all said that they would be ready.

Over the next hour the conversation continued, with Kiziah telling tales of Sahael, and admonishing them about being careful if they tried to escape. The consequences for any slave were extremely severe.

Kiziah knew from experience.

Oadira looked over Kiziah's body, seeing all the scars and deformities left over from her attempts at escape. Oadira listened to her explain that before she became a maidservant, a witan man had raped and impregnated her. She gave birth to a baby girl, but she didn't want such a beautiful little thing to become a sex slave, so she placed her hands over her tiny nose and mouth, taking the life out of the newborn. She ran away under cover of darkness; unfortunately, the baby's witan father caught her. He dragged her by her long hair back to his plantation. The witan man and his friends held her down as they cut off her ears, with all thirty-seven of them having their way with her. After they had finished, they beat her body to near death.

Oadira could see her rubbing the side of her head where her ears would have been.

Kiziah explained that despite all of that, she had not stopped trying to escape, and when the time was right, she would attempt it again.

How could a woman so strong have gone through so much?

"Dit is Kiziah se tyd," one of the girls said in reply to the tale. "It is Kiziah's time."

"Time to escape," another whispered.

"Dit is Kiziah se tyd," Oadira agreed. "Let's get some sleep. We have a big day ahead of us."

CHAPTER III

THE ROYAL RUMBLE

Aban City, El Djem Colosseum

The *Nightingale* sailed silently along the private river headed to Aban City. At midday, they finally arrived. Built from gleaming white and cream stones, Aban bustled with activity. The docks were full of ships, with the parapets of the city wall teeming with people running here and there in preparation for the games.

Oadira, the Madame, Delphine, Martha, and Lord Commander Natas boarded a carriage to the city's main square. Up to this point, Oadira kept her emotions in check. Being so close to Natas made her skin crawl. For his part, Natas paid no attention to her. She was just another slave to him.

Although she yearned for the opportunity to lash out at every witan she encountered, she didn't. Instead, she sat in the carriage, watching more of her brethren in obsidian chains, completely subdued as if they accepted their bondage. She knew the magical obsidian chains had a severe effect on their psyche, causing them to remain supine even when subjected to wrongdoing.

The Madame noticed Oadira's fixation on the shiny cuffs.

"Those obsidian chains are expensive," Lalaurie said, nodding toward Natas. "It's impressive you have so many of them here, Lord Commander. We're forced to use a lesser form of obsidian on our estate. The slaves on my plantation are docile and do their jobs on command, but I'm sure yours are far more servile, as is their station in life."

Natas nodded his head, barely listening to the woman. His eyes were also focused on the world outside the window, though what he was thinking Oadira could only guess.

Oadira maintained her composure. Ever since last night when Kiziah had mentioned the bracelet and how it amplified the emotions of the women around her, Oadira had become so much more aware of its effects. Every woman she saw seemed to radiate their feelings in her direction, especially the slaves. Their pain clawed at her. Racial battle fatigue began to set in, and she wanted to do something about it but didn't know how. Looking out of the carriage window, she observed the city and all the slaves they passed.

After several hours traveling on the cobblestone and the dirt roads, they finally pulled up outside of the colosseum of El Djem, home of the Royal Rumble. The stadium measured two hundred meters long, two hundred meters wide, and one hundred meters in height. Its brilliant ivory color reflected the bright sun, making it almost unbearable to look at for more than a few seconds. The arena could seat 250,000 spectators for various events, including gladiator contests, animal hunts, and reenactments of famous battles. There were even mock sea battles as they flooded the colosseum with water. It was said that at times they would have magicians perform spectacular light shows with their artes and dazzle the entire city. Thousands from far and wide came to bear witness to the year's main event, the Royal Rumble.

Oadira stepped out of the carriage, gasping at the sight of

the massive colosseum. She tilted her head skyward as she took in the grand height of the calcite and concrete structure that stood before her. When she brought her head down, the dismal scene across the street starkly juxtaposed the magnificent beauty of the colosseum.

A piercing scene of poverty and suffering met her gaze. A group of slaves in pronged collars were under heavy guard with leg irons on their feet. Twenty witans half their size and stature surrounding them with swords and spears.

I hope that they will free themselves of their oppressors' chains and bring wrath down upon them one day, whispered Oadira to herself.

One of the enslaved men gasped and pointed at Oadira. His eyes fell on her bracelet and rings.

"Die tyd is nou," he said with a bow. One of the guards hit him in the back of the leg with his spear to shut him up.

How is now the time? Oadira questioned. He had seen her bracelet, and just as Kiziah had said, it gave the man hope.

A few paces away from the slaves stood a variety of trainers and their wrestlers. All the guards were witans except one instructor, whose chocolate complexion made him stick out from the rest. His seven-foot gargantuan size proved that he had earned his freedom as the undefeated Royal Rumble champion. After earning his freedom, the man had gone on to become a ten-time champion. He became a trainer to coach and develop other wrestlers. This allowed him to have complete mobility to move freely throughout the inner provinces despite the racial tensions he encountered daily.

Oadira's eyes caught the attention of the trainer's wrestler, who stood ten feet tall and was bald, with white, ivory teeth that glistened when the sun hit them. The wrestler's chiseled and well-defined body made everyone marvel as they passed.

Delphine stepped next to Oadira and sneered at the trainers and wrestlers.

"The wrestlers are eager to please the crowd and their coaches, in hopes of winning their freedom once again," Delphine chuckled. "Do you believe they were free once? What a waste. When enslaved wrestlers are captured as free men, they'll do whatever it takes to regain their freedom. They don't deserve it."

Delphine spit on the ground and walked away.

Oadira took in the sights of the town and felt the familiar sensation of butterflies in the pit of her stomach as she walked with Madame Lalaurie and her sisters. Lord Commander Natas and the others had already made their way to the colosseum. Suddenly, Oadira felt a warmth and love she hadn't experienced in several years. She looked around, knowing her cousins were somewhere nearby. Her heart raced in anticipation of seeing them once again. She peered through the crowd until she spotted Heziara and Aamira rushing along the cobblestone street excitedly. They both looked strong and healthy, wearing frilly dresses similar to Oadira, like dolls on display in a shop.

In the blink of an eye, the three of them were wrapped in a heartfelt embrace.

"It's good to see you again!" Aamira said.

"Oh my gosh, it's been too long!" Heziara gushed.

"It's good to see the both of you again," Oadira said as the three of them embraced each other tightly.

Martha rolled her eyes and scoffed. "Enjoy it while it lasts."

The sisters ignored Martha's comment and continued to hold each other close. Oadira pulled away first, placed her hands on Heziara's left cheek and Aamira's right cheek. She gazed into their eyes. Tears streaked down their ebony faces. The three sisters looked nearly identical to each other with only subtle differences to distinguish between them. They had the same long braided hair that stretched to the middle of their backs, but Oadira's hair contained a hint of blue, Aamira's held a slight tinge of green, and Heziara's retained a bit of gray.

"How have you been?" Oadira asked quietly.

"Safe, but miserable," Heziara answered. *"I will say the rest without speaking, to keep us safe."*

"Agreed," Oadira replied. It had been a long time since she had heard another voice in her head, and she relished the feeling of unity it provided between herself and her cousins. *"It has been too long since I have communicated telepathically. I have missed you both so much."*

"We are to be sold to the wrestlers," Aamira whispered telepathically. *"Madame Delphine blathers when she's drunk. I've known for weeks. They've been blackmailed by someone regarding a murder they all took part in."*

"I know of the murder," Oadira confirmed. *"I was there when it happened many years ago. It finally came back to haunt them."*

"And us, apparently," Aamira continued. *"I've wanted to run away, but I couldn't do it without the two of you."*

"We cannot let them do this to us," Oadira replied.

Aamira pulled their foreheads together, making sure they were touching. Speaking in a whisper, she said, *"We all need to continue playing along until an opportunity presents itself that we can take advantage of, as we continue to figure out a way. I feel like Nergal and the seers of old will guide us."*

The three princesses nodded in unison.

"I have been planning my escape for the past week as well," Oadira added. *"Ever since I found out about the Madame's plan. Like you. Aamira, I couldn't do it alone. I wanted you both beside me. Now I want our people beside me too. I pray for their salvation."*

"Let's just make the best out of the time we have together," Heziara said as small tears fell from her left eye.

"This might be our last time together and the last time we see each other," Oadira said as she made eye contact with Aamira and Heziara.

"Once we are sold off and married to one of these brutes, there is no way to know how our lives will unfold," Aamira said.

"It won't come to that," Oadira said out loud to add force to her words. "We will be free. Our people will be free. Trust in that."

"Let's get going. Madame, Martha, and Delphine are finishing up negotiations and entering the colosseum," Heziara said, wiping her eyes.

"We need to enter with them to avoid any trouble," Oadira warned.

Delphine turned back to address Oadira, Aamira, and Heziara, who were holding hands and following closely behind. "Come!" she barked rudely. "We don't want to keep the suitors waiting."

A young Black girl walked the group inside the colosseum, escorting them to their ringside seats. Oadira had never sat this close before where she could look down mere feet from the fighters. She would likely be able to hear their bones breaking; a thought that brought her no joy.

The energy inside the colosseum burst with excitement. Permeating the air was the intense smell of body odor, sweat, and alcohol on the breaths of those they passed on the way to their seats. The celebration they were preparing to watch was anything but a standard sporting event. The brutality on display would be unappetizing in the extreme. Plus, in this circumstance, the competition would determine who would impregnate the three princesses. Their entire lives had been boiled down to how they could procreate and earn money for their witan benefactors.

Many of the wrestlers stood outside the ring, gazing upon where they would fight and likely die, thinking of their victory, or sizing up other wrestlers. Tension, testosterone, and the smell of bodily fluids filled the arena. It made Oadira queasy as her vision blurred slightly. Nerves in her stomach reached their angry tendrils all the way to the back of her throat. She felt as if she would vomit. Luckily, with her sisters on the right and left of her, clasping her hands, she got through the traumatic ordeal.

Something would happen that would allow for her escape. Not just her, but her sisters, and the slave women as well. The Gods would watch over them.

They had to.

After a few minutes, Lord Commander Natas walked down the aisle, flanked by dignitaries in colorful robes. Oadira didn't recognize many of them, but she had met President Tiberius on several occasions before. He was a tall lean man, much taller than the average witan, powerfully built but now well past his prime. White hair fell to his shoulders. He was dressed in fine clothing, an echo of the station he held in society. Oadira knew that President Tiberius was responsible for the ships providing naval control over the waters of Western and Eastern Aarde. His sitting with Natas was not a coincidence. He nodded to the princess as he sat down in front of them, commenting to Natas about how the fighters looked particularly strong this year. Natas agreed and went on a diatribe about breeding the right kinds of wrestlers for the right kinds of tournaments.

As they talked, another man approached, hooded in a black cloak darker than anything Oadira had ever seen. It was as if no light reflected off the fabric. He leaned next to Natas and whispered something in his ear. Natas nodded his head toward Oadira and her cousins. The man turned and stared at the three princesses. While his face was shadowed so Oadira couldn't see even the color of his skin, his eyes seemed to glow a pale orange. He stared for a few more seconds before shaking his head, whispering to Natas again, and walking back the way he came.

Who was that? Aamira asked. *He sent chills up my spine.*

I've never seen a cloak like that before, Heziara replied.

Best not to worry too much about it, Oadira mused. *Between Natas, these witan overlords, and the Lalaurie sisters, sinister people are going to be like wheat in the fields at harvest time.*

As everyone sat in their seats, a trainer walked past them with his wrestler. He sat down right beside Madame Lalaurie with Martha and Delphine on his left. The young wrestler with him turned and gave a quick nod to the young princesses.

Oadira recognized the wrestler. His features were older, but he still held the young energy she had witnessed years before on the slave ships. He was Nezikiah, a young man who was sexually violated by Lynch's sailors.

Oadira's eyes grew heavy, and her heart raced as the cries became deafening. Her hands began to shake. Whether it was the realization that she recognized the wrestler and the unpleasant memories that came with it, or her growing understanding of the emotions she felt from the people around her, Oadira began to sense feelings that didn't belong to her. It was as if the emotions of all the women in the stadium, slaves and freed alike, invaded her thoughts and threatened to crush her mind. Excitement, apprehension, lust, fear, pride, all of it crushed her senses.

"Oadira, are you alright?" Aamira whispered.

"It's…too much," Oadira moaned.

Aamira shook Oadira's wrist and tried to snap her out of it while Heziara looked around inconspicuously to ensure no one else was watching.

"Oadira!" Aamira whispered harshly into her mind. *"Come on, snap out of it!"*

"I'm…alright," Oadira said, eyes blinking open as the moment seemed to pass.

Madame Lalaurie turned to them and glared. "Don't embarrass me! Just sit there and keep your mouths shut!"

Oadira looked at Aamira. "That's the young boy that Captain Lynch and his crew sodomized and humiliated. Remember? On the ship? His name was Nezikiah."

"I have spent the last fifteen years trying to forget about the horrible things I saw on Captain Lynch's ship," Aamira said.

The three of them stared at the trainer and his wrestler.

The black trainer stood at the ringside with his enormous size in full view. The coach stood six feet, ten inches and weighed over 260 pounds; he was a marvel to look at. Where most of the trainers were scarred from years of fighting, with thick gouges on their faces and necks from their time in the arena, this wrestling instructor looked unblemished. His garb made him stand out as well. The other instructors wore simple canvas robes with few bracelets or rings to speak of. Nezikiah's on the other hand wore fine silver armor over his shoulders and chest, green robes flowing in the slight breeze. All the other trainers and wrestlers looked at him with a sense of awe, admiring his body and intellect as they gazed at the man.

Who was this man? Oadira had never seen him at the

Rumble before. He seemed as important as Natas, but with a quiet dignity lost on the evil conqueror.

Matches began, and all eyes focused on the arena. The audience observed various fighting styles of wrestling from different parts of Alkebulan and throughout Aarde that reflected their different cultures and pride.

"The wrestling ring provides these wrestlers a place of solace and comfort and an escape from the cruelties of Aarde," Madame Lalaurie said as she made eye contact with Aamira, Oadira, and Heziara. "This is a mercy for them. Remember, what I've done for you, and what I do today, is a mercy."

Several trainers and fighters crowded around the ring. A lean witan man, no taller than five feet, entered through the ropes, wearing ill-fitting clothes and oversized sandals. His oily hair lay flat on his head, covering his forehead and ears. His feeble stature confused Oadira as she wondered what a small witan like him would do in a ring that was soon to become the site of bloodshed and death.

Oadira was shocked when an unnaturally loud and deep voice bellowed from the small witan. "Ladies and gentlemen!" he shouted. The words were magically amplified, though how he was doing it escaped Oadira's understanding. "Welcome to the Fiftieth Annual Royal Rumble! A spectacle like no other! The biggest, strongest, and baddest of bulls have come here to achieve victory over all rivals! I'd like to offer a special round of applause for last year's champion, Demarco, as he returns to show his dominance!"

The crowd cheered as Demarco, a black albino built like a rhinoceros, raised his left hand to excite the mob. The wrestler's pigment didn't affect his eyes or his hair; he had golden dreadlocks with almond skin. The wrestler's facial features resembled those of the Egyptians and the Sahaelians. He stood seven feet tall, nearly five inches shorter than Nezikiah; he was the current champion wrestler and had turquoise-colored eyes and tattoos. He then performed several backflips, throwing the throng into a frenzy as his bronze skin reflected the bright sun overhead.

"The rules of the game are simple: The majority of these coons will team up against other coons. If a coon is thrown over the top of the rope, hits the solid spiky pavement, and is knocked unconscious, or of course is killed by their opponent, they are disqualified and subsequently out of the competition if they can't get back inside the ring within fifteen seconds. Your coons will fight until their final breath! The last bull standing will be our new reigning Royal Rumble champion!"

The crowd roared with excitement.

"This isn't about a matter of pride, dear spectators," the announcer continued. "These brave and powerful men compete for breeding rights and their choice of women. Wouldn't we all want that privilege? They fight here now for pleasure later, and to create the next generation of fighters. It's an opportunity to enjoy the spoils of their hard work for the next twelve months in hopes of one day competing for their freedom!

"Let the battle begin!" the announcer shouted. His shoulders slumped, and he exited the ring, disappearing into the audience.

The wrestlers amped themselves up by making their way down the aisles and circling the ring. Fifty wrestlers, adrenaline pumping and testosterone overflowing, would soon crowd the small, square space.

"I hate it here," Aamira said. "The crowd's cheers are deafening. I can barely hear."

DING! DING! DING! At the sound of the bell, all fifty wrestlers entered the ring at once.

"The Royal Rumble has begun," Oadira said with a look of

disgust on her face. Every year she sat here next to Madame Lalaurie and watched the brutality. Every year she longed to return home to the estate. Now, if she couldn't escape, she would be saddled to some debased wrestler and become nothing more than breeding stock for a rich witan.

After an hour had passed, half of the fifty wrestlers had been disqualified or killed; many wrestlers gave up through submission restraints, such as the sleeper hold, the lion tamer, and the sharpshooter. Natural-born Alkebulans used finishing moves such as the figure-four leg lock, the torture rack, and the squeeze.

A few wrestlers used moves from across the ring and jumping from the top of the ropes, which forced several combatants into submission using their impressive acrobatic displays of superior athleticism, strength, and agility.

Each passing hour the fights became more and more ferocious.

After nearly five hours, less than ten wrestlers remained in the ring. The crowd had grown wild and boisterous. Two fighters began to stand out from the rest in Oadira's eyes: Demarco, the returning champion, and the Wiru boy who Oadira had recognized, Nezikiah. She had seen him more than once in her dream as he was raped by men on Lynch's ship. He was no longer the young boy who had been tasked with her protection. Now, the tall, muscular man was a vicious fighter, seemingly every bit as cruel as the men from Lynch's ship. She couldn't deny his skill and stamina, however.

Nezikiah took several blows to his chest area, bringing him to his knees. In this vulnerable position, another wrestler ran to the ropes to get momentum to bring him to the mat. Nezikiah caught the wrestler by the thighs, stood up, and slammed him on the ring mat, shattering his back into pieces. The other wrestlers stood stunned. The crowd dropped into complete silence.

Taking advantage of this opportunity, Nezikiah snatched another wrestler from midair, attempting a finishing move on an unconscious warrior lying on the canvas. He executed a spinning neck breaker, snapping the fighter's spine and cracking his back into two pieces.

"That was a ruthless move!" the announcer cried. "That right there is Nezikiah! He was transported on the slave ships from Sahael itself, with the strength and ferocity of his savage bloodline!"

The other wrestlers backed off as Nezikiah performed a devastating leg drop on a competitor's chest, rendering him unconscious. He then crushed the man's ribs, puncturing the fighter's heart with his own rib bones. The combatant spit up blood and choked to death in a series of croaks.

The crowd erupted in response to the blatant violence. Patrons of the colosseum grew insatiable and started chanting the Nezikiah name out loud.

"Nezikiah! Nezikiah! Nezikiah! Nezikiah!"

Nezikiah caught another wrestler in midair who foolishly spring-shot himself off the ropes attempting to build enough momentum to take him down. Spinning around, Nezikiah grabbed the incoming wrestler around the neck with his thighs and executed a front-face, inverted headlock. Falling to the mat, he drove the wrestler's head into the ground. The wrestler's back shattered, his spine snapped, and his skull cracked.

Oadira couldn't believe what she was seeing. The young boy who had stood by them during their brutal journey across the sea had been turned into a brutal killing machine. He seemed to take life without the slightest thought or hesitancy. It disgusted her.

The crowd continued to get louder and louder, indifferent to Oadira's disgust. Nezikiah threw another wrestler off the ropes, sling-shotting his opponent back, which enabled Nezikiah to lunge forward with exceptional force and perform a technique called the spear, which crushes the wrestler's pelvic area, permanently bringing him down onto the canvas.

"Ten wrestlers are all that remain in the ring," the announcer shouted through the colosseum. His amplified voice seemed every bit as excited as the 250,000 other spectators.

"The wrestlers are forming into two teams," he continued. As he spoke, colosseum workers rushed the arena, grabbing at large valves linked to cisterns and piping that led back toward the arena walls. "They are doing this out of survival! five wrestlers against five wrestlers. It appears that the colosseum stadium staff has entered the arena area. They are opening the ocean valves to fill the center of the colosseum with fresh saltwater. This is what you've been waiting for, citizens of Aarde! As you can see, the arena floods almost instantly! That is why we here in the city of Aban are superior to all other races. Our engineering is unlike anything in the world. Oh, look at that! The colosseum workers have now released several species of sharks in the water outside of the ring. They've put over thirty tiger sharks, bull sharks, bronze whaler sharks, and white-tip sharks in the water!"

The boisterous crowd cheered as sharks tore into the flesh of the dead wrestlers and those trying to swim away. Then they started circling and waiting to prey on any of the wrestlers thrown into the waters from the top ropes. 250,000 people screamed at the top of their lungs, cheering on their favorite wrestlers.

Lord Commander Natas's special guests and dignitaries cheered right along with them. Occasionally Oadira would catch them laughing about something or commenting on the prowess of the fighters.

"These games are a wonderful sight, seeing these black animals beat on each other for our entertainment," President

Tiberius said. "It's so easy to get them to kill each other. As a child everyone always said Sahael was such a powerful nation. They proved to be anything but, didn't they, Lord Commander?"

"I do what I can for the good of Aard," Natas replied, white teeth shining against his dark skin.

President Tiberius looked over to his three colonial generals who were enjoying the Royal Rumble, oblivious to their leader. "It's time," the president said, tapping several of them on the shoulder. "I need the three of you to leave and make your way to the colonies. The fight's almost about over once the sharks get involved."

The three colonial generals got up, looks of disappointment on their faces, and awaited President Tiberius's orders. They were all dressed similar to the president, with their white robes and golden accents. One of them even had gold leaf dotted around his eyes as if he were blessed with gilded accents.

"General Vipsanius," President Tiberius continued. "You are to take control of the Lucedale colony. General Scipio, you are to take control of the Vannadale colony. General Constantine, you are to take control of the Abingdale colony."

Before exiting, the generals shouted to their favorite wrestlers, gave them all a thumbs up, and made their way out of the stadium.

The crowd roared as the fight continued. Demarco stomped on another wrestler's neck and crushed his windpipe. For a second, he and Nezikiah looked at each other, but made no move to single each other out.

Not yet.

A wrestler lunged toward Nezikiah, placing him in a headlock, and brought him down to the mat. He repeatedly hit Nezikiah with heavy blows to his head, cracking his ribs as he tried squeezing the life out of him. Nezikiah bled from his mouth, lips, and ears. He appeared tired and frustrated despite his astounding victories up to this point.

To the excitement and the roar of the colosseum crowd, Nezikiah lifted his opponent off the mat, and threw him over the ropes into the water now roiling in the colosseum. Sharks attacked immediately and ravished the flesh from his bones.

The crowd, now in a complete frenzy, screamed with passion and amazement.

Nezikiah winced and gasped with each movement he made. The right and left sides of his torso were deep purple. He fell to his knees, laboring to breathe efficiently. Two of the remaining wrestlers saw their chance. They attacked Nezikiah simultaneously.

Nezikiah quickly reacted by pirouetting in a complete circle, grabbing each wrestler by the neck, and tossing them out of the ring and into the water.

While Nezikiah caught his breath, four other contestants met their fates either from the sharks or the brutal fists of the other wrestlers.

Now only three fighters remained.

One of the final two wrestlers rushed Nezikiah from behind.

Nezikiah quickly grabbed the body of a dead wrestler still in the ring and hurled it behind him. His charging opponent, caught by surprise, buckled under the weight of the dead man and collapsed like a pretzel, head bending back to the point it touched his heels.

Two wrestlers remained: Nezikiah and the previous Royal Rumble champion, the albino Demarco.

Turning away from Nezikiah, Demarco took the bodies of the dead wrestlers and threw them outside the ring, feeding the sharks and intensifying the crowd.

"Are you ready?" Demarco shouted as he made eye contact with Nezikiah.

Nezikiah nodded his head in agreement, charging toward Demarco. They hit each other with a ferocity that bordered on barbaric. The two men punched, clawed, and pushed. Just as it seemed Demarco might have the upper hand, Nezikiah spit blood in his eye, catching the albino by surprise. With a punishing twist, Nezikiah appeared to have dislocated Demarco's shoulder before forcing him over the ropes and into the water.

Sharks swarmed, screams echoed through the arena, until finally silence reigned.

Demarco never resurfaced.

A thunderous roar exploded from the colosseum, signifying Nezikiah's victory.

As the last man standing and new champion of the Fiftieth Annual Royal Rumble, Nezikiah dropped to his knees on the mat and placed both arms in the air in celebration of his achievement. A tiny boat retrieved Nezikiah from the ring and took him to rest and recover inside the luxurious tent he shared with his trainer.

"Not a bad match at all," President Tiberius said to Natas. I thought Demarco would be a repeat winner, but it's always good to spread the sperm around."

Natas stood and motioned for the president to follow him. "It doesn't matter who wins. A dog breeds with a dog. Whether the beast has spots or stripes is not my concern. Let us go and congratulate our victor."

The two men nodded to Nezikiah's trainer as they walked toward the exit. The coach, dark bald head glistening with a fine sheen of sweat, sat just to the right of the three princesses. He turned to face Madame Lalaurie and her sisters. He nodded to them and stood.

"There you have it," he said, adjusting the gauntlets on the end of his shirt sleeves. "My wrestler has shown great stamina, strength, and courage. He will provide strong boys by the blessings of Ibeji to help carry on a strong lineage of champion wrestlers."

The Madame rose from her seat and gave a slight curtsy. "I can clearly see that your bull paired with my three virgins would make a wrestling dynasty."

So, that was it, Oadira thought. She and her sisters would be given to Nezikiah as a reward. She wondered how much the fancy trainer would pay to have them. Children from three virgins of their physical stature, coupled with a champion wrestler, would fetch an astronomical price, like a pure-breed Mastiff, only disposable.

No, Oadira and her sisters were together now. Within the next few hours, they would make their escape and trust in the God's of their ancestors to protect them.

Madame Lalaurie turned back to the young women and signaled with her hand for them to rise. Heziara, Aamira, and Oadira rose to their feet but kept their heads bowed.

"It seems you were right," Lalaurie sighed. "I wondered how you were so confident in your victory, but now it seems it was inevitable. Your wrestler delivered against all odds. As has been arranged with the Rumble Regents, your bull will be given access to my family's three virgins on our estates in Lucedale, Vannadale, and Abingdale."

"These three young women are the Lalaurie family's purest prized virgins," Martha said in an unpleasant tone. She grabbed Aamira by the chin and squeezed her cheeks, so her lips opened slightly. "Look at their teeth; perfect and white. That alone proves their health and value. Along with access to them, I give you this pass, allowing you unlimited access to our estates for the next twelve months until the Fifty-First Annual Royal Rumble." She handed the trainer a collection of documents wrapped in a leather binder.

The trainer took the folder and smiled at the girls. It wasn't a snide or angry smile like Oadira was so used to seeing from men like this. It seemed almost kind, as if he understood what the women would soon suffer.

"Please follow me, ladies," the trainer said, pointing to an archway just beyond the stadium's seats. "If the Lalaurie sisters would stay here for a moment, I'd love to introduce the virgins to their breeding partner."

Madame Lalaurie frowned. "This is unorthodox, especially since payment---"

"You have nothing to worry about," the trainer interrupted. "Your girls will be perfectly safe." He reached his chestnut hand to take Madame Lalaurie's old, wrinkled one and brought it to his lips. "You have my word that payment will be made, and the girls will be safe."

Madame Lalaurie nodded in agreement to his request, cheeks suddenly flushed. As the trainer led the princesses toward the archway, Oadira heard the Lalaurie sisters squabbling.

"How could you allow a black man the audacity to bring his Nigger lips your skin?" Delphine said, looking utterly disgusted.

Oadira knew Madame Lalaurie had enjoyed 'nigger lips' on the skin of more than just her hands, so Delphine's objection seemed laughable.

The trainer led them outside where a crowd had gathered in

the afternoon sun. Nezikiah stood before Lord Commander Natas himself, surrounded by soldiers, hangers-on, and the duly elected president from the Dales.

"That was a great display of power, strength, and persistence," Lord Commander Natas said. "Your prize is not only the honor of your victory, but the chance to share your strength with the next generation."

Oadira started fidgeting with her clothes and scratching her arms. Her stomach almost knotted up again, forcing her to put her hand on her gut to prevent herself from dry heaving. Outside the Colosseum, food wagons and general seating for spectators, guests, and visitors lined the walls. Could they escape now with so many people around? Perhaps hide under the bleachers or behind the vender stalls? Could she grab her sisters' hands and disappear into the crowd unnoticed?

Of course not. They were taller than half the men present. They wouldn't blend in no matter where they went, especially in broad daylight. Could they wait till nightfall? Would the brute Nezikiah have his way with them before that? She wanted to run and never look back, charge into the crowd and take her chances, but she looked at Aamira and Heziara and knew she couldn't abandon them.

"Take this warrior to his tent for some rest," Natas shouted to the cheers of the hundreds of people pressing to get a closer look at the victorious wrestler. Nezikiah nodded at the Lord Commander, never saying a word, and stepped toward his trainer and the three princesses.

"I'd like to introduce myself," the trainer said to the girls. "My name is Solomon, the Protector of Aarde. Nezikiah will escort you young ladies to my private tent. And do not worry, no harm will come to you, nor will Nezikiah touch or molest you in any way. I merely wish to speak with you, if that is alright."

Oadira looked at her sisters. They had no reason to trust this man.

“Where is your tent?” Oadira asked.

“On the north side of the colosseum,” Solomon replied. “Near the underground tunnels that run to the marketplace.”

The underground tunnels. Oadira had never used them personally, but they seemed like the perfect escape route. She and her sisters could reach the Aloe River under the mountains north of the city quickly enough. It would be best to follow along for now.

Freedom was close. She could feel it.

Long corridors and staircases led them to the north. After a few minutes, Oadira risked speaking with her sisters through telepathy.

“Our chance is soon, sisters. We will flee to the north. If this Nezikiah attempts to touch us, we will defend ourselves. Hopefully as night falls, we can sneak away. Trust in the Gods.”

“Trust in the Gods,” Aamira and Heziara responded.

Eventually Nezikiah led them into the courtyard beyond the primary market of Aban. Several large, luxurious tents filled the space while servants ran here and there for their masters.

Once inside the tent, Nezikiah quietly positioned himself in a corner with his hands clasped in front of him. The three princesses stood in the center on a lion-skin rug. Lamps hung from wooden support beams above, flickering in the air currents. The tent was spacious and had two rooms, one with two beds and another with a table, chairs, stools, and a metal, wood-burning stove to keep warm. Bint-El-Sudan incense burned, wafting through the entire tent with an aroma that put people at ease.

Oadira glanced over at Nezikiah. His nature seemed so calm now. Just moments ago, he was a raging wrestler choking the life out of grown men in front of the whole colosseum.

After about 15 minutes, the trainer entered the tent while several albino midwives waited outside. As he looked at the princesses, his shoulders suddenly slumped. He seemed relieved, as if he could let down his guard like his code posturing and switching were no longer needed.

"How are you all doing?" Solomon asked with an enormous sigh of relief.

"We are doing well," answered the three cousins in unison, as if prepared for the question.

"It is okay to express how you all truly feel," the trainer said candidly.

The girls were still reluctant, not knowing if they could trust the trainer or not.

"Do the three of you know why you are here this evening?" Solomon asked.

Oadira looked at her cousins without knowing what to say; all they could do was shake their heads in response.

"The three of you are here because I needed three pure virgins, hand-selected for my championship wrestler Nezikiah," the trainer said as he motioned his hand toward his protégé, prompting him to move closer to the group.

"We remember who you are," Oadira said. "You were humiliated in front of everyone captive on the *Nightingale*."

For a moment Oadira feared she should have remained quiet, but her anger at everything that had happened over the past few days boiled inside her. Her heart raced as she waited for a response.

Nezikiah nodded in agreement.

"As I said before, my name is Solomon," the trainer

continued. “I am keeper of the histories and protector of Sahael. Nezikiah can’t speak; his tongue was cut out for being one of the people who helped protect you three on the *Nightingale*. I purchased Nezikiah from Captain Lynch and taught him sign language.”

A servant entered and brought Solomon a glass of purple liquid. He took a sip and nodded toward the princesses.

“It has taken a lot of patience and time to find all three of you. It has taken even more time to get you all in one location. I have employed thousands of runaway slaves—runaways that escaped your respective plantations and estates—to share with me information about your whereabouts in the colonies. My Educators have done a wonderful job to get you all here.”

“What do you mean, ‘get us here?” Oadira asked.

“We were brought by our mistresses,” Heziara added. “They owe a debt, and we are the price, apparently.”

Solomon smiled. “And who do you think was blackmailing the Lalaurie sisters?”

The flap over the tent door rustled as the wind blew outside. Other than that, no one made a sound.

“Surprised?” Solomon asked. “A lot of effort has been put forth to bring you three here. I hope that before you run off to the north at nightfall and hide in the woods, you’ll at least hear what I have to say.”

Impossible! How could this man know what Oadira had spoken only in her mind? How could he have guessed their thoughts?

“The primary purpose of this meeting is twofold,” Solomon continued. “I needed to see if you all had kept your virtue intact. I also needed to ensure Madame Lalaurie’s breeding rights would have no complications with my championship wrestler.

"But this whole thing is an act. Although it matters that the three of you are pure—it will make Ibeji bless you more now than ever—just play along and follow my instructions. Some of what is about to happen will be uncomfortable for you, but know it is necessary. What I am doing is customary, to buy us a lot of time to speak. From there, I would speak with you regarding your freedom."

The word 'freedom' excited Oadira. This man made it sound like they could only have it through him. She wanted to scratch his face and run off right then and there.

Solomon stared at Oadira, as if her thoughts were written on her face. "Several midwives are going to enter my tent and confirm that your hymens are intact. I have to do this to cover my bases and not bring any negative attention to any of you or me. These are the colosseum rules, regulations, and guidelines."

"Do we even have a choice?" Oadira asked.

"There is always a choice, I will not authorize it unless the three of you consent," Solomon said. "But I promise you, this moment of discomfort will allow us freedoms that we otherwise will lose. Do you understand?"

"Heziara, Aamira, what do you think?" Oadira asked.

"Let's do it," they said simultaneously. Her cousins were emotionless, as if they were resigned to their fates.

"Very good," Solomon nodded. "Nezikiah and I will step out of the tent and wait for the albino midwives to finish their duty."

As Solomon and the wrestler exited, three albino midwives dressed in white ceremonial robes entered. They were tall, but weak and thin. If needed, Oadira and her sisters could overpower them easily. Heziara and Aamira simply looked at the floor though, leaving Oadira to her silent anger. After thirty minutes of examination, the pale midwives exited Solomon's private tent.

"All three princesses are pure and untouched," said the head midwife to Solomon as he stepped back inside.

"Thank you," Solomon said to her. "Be sure to pass the documents along that confirm this. Let the Lalaurie sisters know they have been examined." Solomon waved his hand toward a fine wooden chest with silver inlays. "Take this chest of gold to the Lalaurie sisters. It is their full payment. And if anyone wishes to speak with me further, tell them I am making sure my bull and his harem are getting to know each other."

"Yes, my lord," the midwife nodded as she stepped out. Two other servants entered and lifted the heavy chest toward the exit.

Blood rushed to Oadira's face. Had this Solomon been lying to them to keep them from overpowering the skinny and frail midwives and trying to escape? Would they be forced to fight back now?

"Thank you for allowing that intrusion," Solomon said as he pulled over a chair and stood behind it. "The customs of this barbaric land are depressingly vile, but one must step carefully when upsetting the world. And I want to thank the three of you for keeping yourselves pure during these dark times of slavery, sex and organ trafficking. You will need all the blessings you can get, and I know this fact will be a great protection to you."

Oadira didn't know what to think; she moved her feet up and down, shaking her leg and rubbing her hands together. She was overcome with rage. Her vaginal cavity had been violated by the midwives in a way she never expected. The agitation of her spirit caused all three of Nebiriau's bracelets on the women to light up, as did Njiru's rings on their fingers.

"And *that* is what we need to talk about," Solomon said,

pointing at the glowing bracelets. He turned toward Nezikiah. "You need to have your wounds and your ribs tended to. I'll get the albino doctors to sooth your bruises as soon as our meeting is over. For now, go watch for unseen ears."

Nezikiah nodded his head in agreement before walking outside the tent to keep a watchful eye on any unwanted newcomers or eavesdroppers.

Solomon looked at the three young princesses. "You're confused."

"Yes," Oadira said, fists clenching. "You know about our bracelets."

"In truth, anyone who walked in right now would know about your bracelets. I take it they've been glowing more frequently?"

Heziara nodded. "They've always glowed at times, but yes, it happens more often lately."

"What do you want?" Oadira interrupted. "You made it sound like we wanted to escape to the north once night fell."

"Wasn't that what you said to each other as Nezikiah was leading you to this tent?" Solomon asked. He pointed to his right temple. "Not everyone hears with their ears, don't you know?"

Heart thumping in her chest, Oadira's nostrils flared. "Who are you? What is this about?"

"The Signs of the Times are upon us," Solomon said with seriousness on his face.

The princesses remained quiet. The phrase meant nothing to Oadira, and she assumed it meant nothing to Heziara or Aamira either.

"The Signs of the Times?" she asked, breaking the silence.

"It has been said that the Black Madonna's will emerge

during the Signs of the Times after Deliquesce's seal has been removed," Solomon said.

"Deliquesce's seal? Black Madonna's? What does that even mean?" Aamira asked.

Solomon nodded. "The three of you are the Black Madonna's that represent the ancient pillars of Sahael destined to usher in the Signs of the Times through your wombs; with Ibeji's blessings, your daughters, sons, grandsons, and granddaughters will be highly favored in the eyes of Obatala and his wife, Ishtar."

Solomon took a deep breath.

"Would you like to know more?"

CHAPTER IV

SOLOMON'S COUNSEL

Aban Province, Aban City

Solomon leaned forward against the chair, looking Oadira, Aamira, and Heziara directly in the eyes. His green robes seemed to billow around him.

"There are four of you, each from one of the Chosen Bloodlines," he said.

"There are only three of us," Heziara corrected.

"Let us sit," Solomon said. He walked over to the tent wall and pulled chairs over for each of the princesses to use. They were decorative, with red velvet upholstery.

"I'd rather stand," Oadira replied as Heziara and Aamira started to take their seats. The other two princesses stopped as if unsure what to do.

"Better to run and escape, correct?" Solomon asked.

"Something like that."

"Oadira, daughter of Nergal, princess of Sahael. You've been feeling strong emotions lately, haven't you?"

Oadira blinked, fingers twitching.

"And I bet you may have noticed once or twice," Solomon continued as he took his seat in front of the women, "that your eyes have glowed along with your bracelets recently. Blue, right? Does that sound correct? And you, Heziara. You dream of flying with wings of your own, don't you? It's so real because you once had wings, just like your ancestors. Would you all like me to go on?"

Slowly, Oadira took her seat between Heziara and Aamira.

"Thank you," Solomon nodded. He seemed tired but energized, like an antelope that had just outran a pack of hyena. "Let us begin at the beginning. There is a fourth princess. It's not surprising you don't remember her since you were so young when Sahael fell. Her name is Damisiah. She is safe and, hopefully in time, will be freed; the albino wrestler Demarco from the Royal Rumble was supposed to lose and make his way back to Naharis's realm. You may remember that he never returned to the surface of the water once Nezikiah threw him out of the ring. That was by design. We needed it to look like he died with the others. In truth, he swam toward one of the pipes used by the sharks. Everyone will assume he's just another torn up body in the water. I confirmed his survival before I returned to the tent.

"Demarco aims to free the rest of the Demirrian people. Damisiah is safe and hidden among them, right under Lord Commander Natas's nose. Until they are ready to make their way to Sahael, this whole scheme was to free them and get to the three of you."

A fourth princess? Oadira had vague memories of playing with another girl besides Heziara and Aamira before they were slaves, but so much of that life felt like fantasy, she couldn't know what was real and what wasn't.

"What happened to her?" Aamira asked.

"How come the three of us were separated from her?" Heziara questioned. "Will we ever see this Damisiah again?"

"In time, you will," Solomon replied. "How much do you remember from the fall of Sahael?"

The three princesses looked at each other. They hadn't spoken of that night in many years, even telepathically. The pain and confusion were too much to contemplate. Even so, Oadira couldn't deny her dreams.

"I've been dreaming about it over the past few months," she admitted.

"And what have you been dreaming?" Solomon asked.

She began with being held in her mother's arms as they ran into a burning palace and told the tale all the way to their arrival at Londone.

"Your dreams are not fantasy, as you wish them to be," Solomon said, shifting in his seat. "They are memory. You are the last surviving members of an ancient royal and Chosen Bloodline."

"Okay," Aamira said. "We've always known we were princesses. The people on the ship would tell us, and many of the plantation slaves on my estate whisper of it as well. I remember my queen mother bleeding in front of me. But for what bloodline? It was so long ago and it's sometimes hard to remember."

"The four of you are ancient princesses destined to be queens, rulers, empresses, and Ptolemies from a chosen and rare bloodline thought severed," Solomon said with a grin on his face. "Sahael is your ancestral home."

"Sahael is a myth," Oadira said, shaking her head. "Or worse, a lie. If Sahael were real, we wouldn't be slaves, would we? My educators taught me about Sahael, but how could a place with magic and powerful kings and queens be destroyed so easily? How could its people be so humiliated for so long? Sahael is a story that

I don't believe.

"But you've said yourself that you've had multiple flashbacks of Sahael in your dreams," Solomon said. "And what of you, Aamira? Heziara?"

"I have as well," Aamira answered.

"Likewise," Heziara said.

"You see, Oadira? It isn't just you. Search within your minds, your dreams, your nightmares. To help you better remember, touch Nebiriau's bracelets together at the same time. The bracelets will unlock the ancient powers of your bloodlines to help you all remember."

Oadira, Aamira, and Heziara made eye contact with each other.

"Why didn't you tell me you were having dreams?" Oadira spoke to their minds.

"You didn't tell us either," Aamira replied.

"You might as well speak out loud," Solomon said, reaching into his robes and pulling out a dried date. He threw it into his mouth and chewed. "I told you before, not everyone hears only with their ears. And I was serious about touching the bracelets together. If you want to know the truth, touch them all together at the same time."

Oadira looked down at her bracelet. The blue glow had subsided somewhat but continued to radiate palely.

"Now, move your chairs closer in a three-way circle and place your hands on each other's heads," Solomon suggested. "This will allow the ancient authorities in your bloodlines to use transference powers to help you recall events from your past with my assistance."

Solomon stood and walked between Oadira, Aamira, and

Heziara, moving his hands over the top of their heads as if blessing them.

"If you cannot remember now, you will in time have your eyes restored, along with your childhood memories. The three of you, plus Princess Damisiah, possess the only way to get back into Sahael."

"How is that even possible?" Oadira asked.

"What is so important about our memories?" Heziara asked.

"It's not merely your memories," Solomon said, looking down at the girls. "Your memories are important for your personal histories, yes, but within your memories are blood markers, a genetic map that will help the three of you regain entry back into Sahael. The Signs of the Times are upon us, like I said. The four of you must do all that is within your power to get home."

The temperature in the tent seemed to have risen twenty degrees as far as Oadira was concerned. "If my dream is real like you say," she began, "then Sahael burned. The water boiled and the skies turned to poison. The forests are ash and all the wildlife perished. If Sahael is real, it's a wasteland."

Solomon touched their heads one by one softly. "All that you three see and have seen will be understood in time. Do you want to see more? If so, you know what you must do."

The three princesses looked at each other, doubt in their eyes. Would it be worse to know the truth or live the lie? To be a simple slave with strange memories, or to know without a doubt of one's royalty and power, while still being a slave?

"What should we do?" Oadira asked.

"I want to know," Heziara replied. *"I would rather hate the truth than doubt myself ever again."*

In unison, Oadira, Heziara, and Aamira reached out their hands, touching their bracelets together. The jewels glowed with heat and energy.

"Very good," Solomon breathed.

In a flash of memory, the minds of the princesses opened. Fuzzy images of childhood, long since forgotten, became crip and focused. Oadira felt her mother's skin, heard her sing, and watched her kingly father address powerful families from across Sahael. She smelled flowers and rich food, obscured at times by the smell of smoke and death.

"I want to reeducate your minds." Solomon's voice spoke from far away as every memory from their lives became clear. "You must understand the sacred knowledge and intricacies of your ancient blood lineages from the beginning. There is a lot the three of you will unlearn as white supremacy has polluted and corrupted your minds. I will start by telling you who you truly are: Kemites from the last of the Ancient Bloodlines. Your ancestors arrived in Aarde inside of an Orichalcum-made vessel that traversed the universe disguised as an asteroid. Orichalcum is an eternal mineral with properties beyond what Aarde was ever meant to sustain. When the vessel arrived here it broke into twelve pieces in the atmosphere, with the main piece crashing in the center of Alkebulan."

"Why did our people leave their original home in the first place?" Oadira asked.

Images of stars and space rock flooded Oadira's mind. She saw tall and beautiful people, their skin dark like hers, navigating the cosmos. Then she saw destruction and suffering as cities larger than anything she could imagine were destroyed by weapons so powerful the planets cracked beneath them.

"The Kemites left in secret during the middle of a civil war," Solomon continued. "They were forced to escape the

Ukáváál and their leaders, Khay and Hemiunu, to save the last of their dying race. The Ukáváál are the most dangerous and destructive race in all of existence. Their very presence is a blight that makes life a mere shadow of death itself."

"What happened after they arrived in their ships?" Aamira asked.

More memories engulfed the princesses. Their minds now completely joined together, sharing each experience and past moment as if they had been their own. Smoke rose from a crash site. Muscles ached as men and women in shiny white bodysuits and flowing robes pushed against debris and collapsed rooms to free themselves from darkness.

"It took several days for them to escape the crash," Solomon said, voice narrating the scenes with fluidity. "Nyathera's asteroid hit in the center of Alkebulan, Horn, and Egypt, creating three floating land structures with a crater of land and water that enhanced and enriched the continent, allowing it to produce unlimited resources. After determining that Aarde was safe, the Kemites removed their space helmets, exposing their copper skin and hair as thick as wool. They were the first people to inhabit Aarde. They named the continent Alkebulan, meaning The Motherland. The Kemites assumed the right of protectorate over the continent, giving the duties of the four realms to the capital at Sahael. Orichalcum made Sahael, Egyptus, Horn, and Alkebulan a technologically advanced country in the Age of Discovery. The mineral has of course remained a secret, keeping its existence hidden to avoid unnecessary wars with witans."

"Wait," Oadira said as she watched these beautiful brown people building Khartoum Palace and the crystal cities of Sahael. "If these Kemites were the first people, were there others that came later?"

"Yes," Solomon answered. "Ishtar and Obatala created

Aarde in eight days, or eight creative cycles we call days. On the eighth day, they prepared to populate it with life. But that was when the Kemites' asteroid pierced the Aarde atmosphere, preventing Ishtar and Obatala from initially sending their people down to Aarde."

Like a flower blooming, human life seemed to suddenly spring up throughout the world. Different races, witans, blacks, and people of varying shades, wandered everywhere on the surface of Aarde, all represented in a gorgeous kaleidoscope of color.

"Centuries later," Solomon's voice resumed, "Ishtar and Obatala sent down more people to inhabit Alkebulan. The Kemites kept to themselves, choosing to protect, serve, and bless their people in every capacity, according to their arrangement. The Kemites lived in Sahael in complete isolation until they had no choice but to emerge from their isolation. Their bloodline was slowly dying due to the local sun, which affected their immortality. To prevent the eradication of their bloodline and to prolong their lineage, they mingled with the four Chosen Bloodlines sent down to Aarde by Ishtar and Obatala. They knew that if they all died, the Alkebulan people would be left vulnerable to unimaginable cruelties to the outside influences of Sahael, Egyptus, Horn, and Alkebulan."

Oadira swayed in her chair, still aware of her body sitting in the tent, but mind touching eons of history. Happiness and pain pulled at her cerebrum as centuries of life raced by too quickly to gain much more than a passing understanding.

"What did the creators of Aarde do about the dying bloodlines of the Kemites?" Oadira asked. "Surely they didn't let them die."

"Ishtar and Obatala descended upon Aarde and met with Kaimana and Kanoa," Solomon answered as the princesses saw beings of pure light and indescribable beauty descend to Aarde and meet with two Sahaelian rulers, tall and strong. "Kaimana and Kanoa were the supreme leaders of the Kemites, and their dying bloodline in Timbuktu. After years of discussion, both decided merging bloodlines was in the best interest to save Sahael, Horn, and Egyptus. Their decisions made the four Chosen Bloodlines eternal, creating an omnipresence in Aarde and Egyptus.

"After an eternal agreement was reached between the Andalusians and the Kemettians, a royal decree was sent out, ordering the new bloodlines to merge. Ishtar and Obatala deemed it necessary to house the newly formed lineages in Sahael and tie their power to the land itself."

"Why did they do this?" Aamira asked.

"Ishtar and Obatala wanted to ensure the protection of all Sahaelians, Hornans, Alkebulans, and Egyptians in Alkebulan. As a result, the four realms produced four princesses, the only girls capable of uniting the eight bloodlines in the four realms. The condition to join the four realms required the four princesses to live in Sahael. It signified that a covenant was reached between the emperors and the empresses to prevent subjugation to Sahael. Princesses were born in every generation, always the first born in the bloodlines, always close in age to each other. Such is the power of the Gods."

Solomon paused and licked his lips before continuing. "But there was a complication."

"Complication?" Heziara asked.

"The four of you were born not close together like previous generations, but on the same day at the exact same time. And you were born blind."

Queens screamed as they gave birth to beautiful baby girls, but instead of colored eyes of blue, green, gray, and turquoise to match their bloodlines, these princesses had no eyes at all, only empty sockets devoid of life.

"We never knew," Oadira whispered. "But we're not blind now. We have eyes. What happened?"

"You were not born in Sahael. Your families lived in the four corners of Alkebulan. Pride allowed the bloodlines to separate, and preservation forced them back together. Kaimana and Kanoa wrote that when the four chosen princesses reached the age of three, you were to visit the capital of Sahael as a part of the agreement to link Sahael to Egyptus through betrothal. Since you were all born at the exact same time, and all of you were blind, it was believed you were the chosen daughters written of anciently. The Sahaelian Congress then ordered your families to stay and reside in Sahael until the four of you reached the age of eighteen.

"As for your blindness, I was summoned by the Sahaelian, Alkebulan, Hornan, and Egyptus Congresses to come to Sahael to restore your eyesight. Your parents brought the four of you before me at only three months old to help restore your sight. I crafted your eyes with approval from the supreme leaders, Kaimana and Kanoa, and the Creators, Ishtar and Obatala, so that you all would have eternal sight," Solomon whispered. "Obatala, Ishtar, Kaimana, and Kanoa blessed the Orichalcum stones with unusual power unbeknownst to the Ancient Bloodlines."

"How did you do it?" Oadira asked.

"Magic is a beautiful thing when done correctly, but it isn't as simple as saying a blessing and restoring sight. I took Orichalcum clay from the ground and crafted eight stones from what remained of Nyathera's asteroid. I morphed the clay into two sapphire stones, two emerald stones, two hematite stones, and two turquoise stones, placing them in your empty eye slots."

Oadira reached up and touched her eyes. She had never before thought much about them. They looked like everyone else's. Suddenly she realized her eyes were more than mere flesh and blood. They were items of eternal power, forged by a mystic blessed by the Gods of light.

"Yes, Oadira," Solomon said in response to her thoughts. "The sapphire stones were serene and as mysterious as the oceans, representing life and vitality throughout Aarde. The emerald stones calm and steadfast as the forest, growing where life was not supposed to in the voided places in Aarde. The gray hematite stones were as pure and clean as the clouds, spreading the seeds of life throughout Aarde. The turquoise stones allowed death to be ruled in the afterlife, hearing the song of the dead sung throughout all of Aarde to remain in their eternal slumber. The true color of your eyes are hidden now, except when your powers begin to manifest, but soon enough they will return to their true shades permanently. When that time arrives, you will usher in the changing of the times."

After several minutes, Oadira, Aamira, and Heziara came out of the transfer. The air in the tent seemed heavy and moist in comparison to the worlds and times they had just witnessed. Oadira slumped in her chair, suddenly exhausted beyond reason. Heziara and Aamira did the same, while Solomon stood over them, skin seemingly glowing with internal power.

"How do you know all of this? Who are you?" Oadira asked, breathing heavily. "You're not just another refuge from Alkebulan like others I've met."

Solomon sat back down and breathed for a moment. He once again looked as any other man would look, with his bald head reflecting the flickering lamps around them.

"Who am I? I am Solomon, third son of Ishtar and Obatala. I am one of their three Andalusian sons sent down to Aarde to help restore equality, balance, and freedom for all."

"Freedom for all," Oadira spat. "You're doing a great job, aren't you?"

"Your anger is not misplaced," Solomon said, voice pained but kind. "My brothers and I serve many people and have great strength, but even we must wait for the signs, which only now are manifesting."

"Where are your other siblings?" Heziara asked. "Are they close? Will they help us escape?"

"My second oldest brother, Horus, came down to save and redeem all Aardian kind from their sins and their fallen state. My oldest brother was cast out of Andalusia and sent into the outer realms of darkness with one-third of the Andalusians who followed him." Solomon's forehead creased as the lines around his eyes deepened with sadness. "Thoughtless rebellion leads to nothing but pain and suffering, particularly when one thinks only of themselves." He breathed deeply and smiled. "Enough about me, let's focus on the three of you. Now is the time for questions. What would you like to know?"

"Our bloodlines come from Sahael?" Heziara asked.

"Yes. You three, and the fourth princess as well, originate from the Kemettian bloodline that helped create Sahael. There were chosen pedigrees that merged to form the Ancient Bloodline. Blessed by Ishtar and Obatala, your lineage provides you all with the ability to regain entry back into your ancestral home of Sahael. The four of you are all that remains of the original eight heritages, as far as anyone knows. Your rare lineages are all that remains of the ancients. Through your wombs, the Ancient Bloodlines of the Nephilim, the Anunnaki, the Hausan, and the Demir can endure. Your wombs will bring forth kings, emperors, and pharaohs who will play a pivotal role in restoring the isolated country of Sahael and bring peace to this tired and wounded world."

"Our wombs?" Oadira asked with a look of bewilderment on her face. "So, even as princesses of these chosen bloodlines, we're only as good as our breeding ability. Is that what you're saying?"

Solomon pointed at their stomachs and said, "Through your wombs, queens, kings, empresses, emperors, princes, and princesses will be endowed with powers from Obatala and Ishtar, the creators of Aarde. I understand your anger because of the way you've been used by your matrons, and how you've seen your people abused, but it is through our posterities that we find true joy. Alone we are nothing, but with our partners, children, grandchildren, and on through the ages, we become the power we were always meant to be. There is a power within the four of your wombs. That power is unlimited, and that power will be unlocked when the four of you least expect it." Solomon looked upon Oadira with eyes as calm as the waters of Lake Lucedale on a clear morning. "Oadira, your eyes are awakened and will one day help you see every inch of the oceans. You will understand the depths of your importance, and experience joy in your children you cannot comprehend right now. For as long as your eyes remain sapphire, you will be able to one day see through all the life that dwells in the waters."

He then looked at Aamira, taking her hands and looking into her eyes. "When your eyes have awakened, Aamira, the minds of the animals on the land will be opened to you, allowing you to see through the senses of all living beasts that roam the lands in Aarde."

Solomon finally moved over in front of Heziara, swaying side to side in his chair. "Heziara, your eyes have awakened and will one day help you see everywhere in the skies, allowing you the ability to see throughout all of Aarde and look down on the beauty of the world like few others ever experience."

"What about Damisiah, our lost cousin? What makes her so special?" Aamira asked curiously.

"Did she have to kill her mother too?" Oadira asked. The

memory, now clear in her mind, brought tears to her eyes. They had just experienced so much, being fed images and thoughts, that only now were the personal details solidifying.

She had killed her own mother. She saw the blood pool in her robes and heard her voice in her head because her mother's vocal cords had been severed.

The sound of weeping filled the tent.

"Shhhh, child," Solomon said, patting Oadira's back like a kind uncle. "Such pain is not yours to bear. You killed no one. The weight of that belongs to someone else. Don't carry it needlessly."

"And who does it belong to?" Oadira asked, voice cracking.

"Lord Commander Natas." Solomon's answer was steady, but his voice grew deeper, as if it was weighed down by secrets and lies. "The time will come for you to learn about him, but now is not that moment. Know only that your mother's deaths are at his feet, and one day he will pay for them, and all the other lives he's taken, in ways no person born of woman can possibly comprehend. He fell to Aarde after betraying the Gods. Now he seeks bodies for his disembodied followers. He conquered Sahael in a single day with power that even I am unfamiliar with. Where he received his strength, I cannot guess. He destroyed the only people who could stand in his way."

Natas.

Oadira had hated him before, but now the memories of him stabbing Ninti under the tree were more than just images from a dream. She hated Natas with a white-hot flame. She wanted him to suffer, and Solomon's words and promise of his punishment were not enough. She wanted him to suffer, yes, but she wanted to be the instrument of his suffering.

"What about Damisiah?" Aamira asked again. "Where is

she?"

"Search your minds, and you'll come to know for yourselves," Solomon said.

"What happens to us now?" Oadira asked. She wiped her tears and sat up straight in the chair. "I know you speak the truth about everything. I can't doubt my own mind and memories. Even so, the witan establishment is powerful and predictable. If they were to find out, they'd destroy everything to keep their way of life, no matter the consequences."

"Your bloodlines are destined to reshape Aarde in the image it was originally supposed to be," Solomon said. "Witan beauty is built on the backs of slaves picking cotton, harvesting tobacco, and mining obsidian ore. An Aarde free of witan persecution will allow people of color the ability to thrive equally. The children of different races will play and thrive together as they once did before the dark days. This is why you all need to get to Sahael for everyone's sake." Solomon stood, facial muscles tensing. "There are those who are looking for you at this moment. They are fully aware and are waiting for the signs. They are in the shadows, waiting for you to fail or slip up or get caught or killed. These are the reasons you must be careful despite the powers you all have. Your powers will need development if you are to be ready when the time comes. Until then, every Sahaelian, every person born with dark skin as well, will be vulnerable to the cruelties of the Narsans who want to spread white supremacy all over Aarde. There is a White Darkness spreading in the hearts of witans. It started in the west with the Narsans and comes from a source not yet identified. This evil that is coming is a whiteness that will cover every inch of Aarde, threatening black lives, and in truth, all life itself. That is why you must make it to Sahael at all costs. Only then will you know what to do and determine what is best for the inhabitants of Sahael."

"Even with our powers you say we'll develop," Oadira said, also standing. "How are we supposed to stop it? If we're all that remains of the ancient bloodlines, how can we stand against an entire society? There are three of us; four if you count the princess we can't even find. You're talking about four people standing against millions."

"You won't be alone," Solomon confirmed. He pulled another date from his robe pocket and threw it in his mouth. "But without the proper leadership, Sahael, Egyptus, Horn, and Alkebulan cannot flourish or prosper. You are the chosen leaders. When the time is right, millions will follow you. Even some who you now see as your oppressors will join your cause and die in the name of the Princesses of Sahael to bring freedom to all."

The weight seemed too heavy to bear. Oadira had wanted freedom for herself and her sisters, maybe the women she had met on Nata's yacht, and the families from her plantation. But millions of people? Leading millions? Fighting millions? Even with her sisters by her side, she felt small and insignificant.

"Everything depends on all four of you getting back to Sahael," Salomon said finally. "Until you do, Aarde will continue to be out of balance, which in return will force White Darkness to spread all over Aarde, creating a reign of unstoppable terror and death. As you find your way to Sahael, you will need to activate the Nairohenge Gates in each of the four realms. It's the only way the four bloodlines can regain entry back into Sahael, paving the way for the first gathering. The Nairohenge Gates will open portals to other realms, allowing the bloodlines to reenter Sahael. It will be magnificent! I will give you a map that details where the gates are hidden and how to access them. You won't be alone in this fight."

He pulled a scroll from his green robes and handed it to Oadira. Solomon took a deep breath.

"It is time for the three of you to put a plan in place and

escape from the living hell. I will aid you in this cause. On your upcoming encounters with Nezikiah, the night before your subsequent scheduled visits, your escapes will be facilitated. Even now the cogs are being put in place, and the madams will be away from the plantations. We will be building secret momentum in the colonies and the outer provinces, bringing more slaves to your cause."

Escape. Before tonight, Oadira had longed for that idea to become a reality, but deep down she knew it was a longshot. Her plan to run north had not been thought out beyond the desire. Now, however, something concrete took shape. She knew who she was. She knew who she could be, and Solomon was helping not only her, but her cousins, to flee toward a brighter tomorrow.

Nothing could stop them.

Solomon rubbed his hands together and pinched the bridge of his nose. "It is time for me to leave now. Our moment together is at an end. In the dark days to come, know you are being watched over. Trust in your power, and soon, you will take your rightful place as leaders of Sahael. War is as constant as death, famine, and pestilence. What they destroy, we will rebuild. Aarde is no virgin to such realities. Oadira, Aamira, and Heziara, what I am about to say will not be repeated."

Solomon moved his chair and knelt on one knee before the princesses.

"When you arrive home, the three of you only have a few months to prepare and plot your escapes from the estates. There's no room for error. Understood?"

"We understand," Heziara said, smiling for the first time since the sisters had met earlier that morning.

"Learn to follow your instincts and trust the power within you from your ancestors," Solomon continued passionately.

"You're not children or powerless slaves, you are of Kemettian royalty. You are queens. You have natural and defiant confidence. Show that you are of Kemettian royalty. I bow before you now, a humble servant of Sahael. Aarde is drowning in white supremacy, slavery, and trafficking of both humans and organs, at the expense of black bodies. Aarde needs you. Teach your sons and daughters the ways of those who have enslaved your people. The three of you have been in captivity since you were little girls, yet your bloodlines have been blessed with immortality, eternal life, and invincibility, as will your offspring. With Damisiah, the four of you are the spark needed to trigger an awakening among the Diaspora, a spark set in motion through the signs triggered by your eyes. On the map I gave you, you will find instructions on where to go. Oadira will head for Iceoth. Aamira, the desert lands of Iff. Heziara, you will fly to the mountainous lands of Nuberia. All has been ordained, and you will find a way."

Heziara stepped toward the kneeling man, face expectant, eyes wide.

"Do I really have wings?" she asked. "Will I really be able to fly all the way to Nuberia?"

"Yes," Solomon smiled. He stood back up and cupped Heziara's cheeks. "My beautiful child. So much has been hidden from you. Your wings are on your shoulder blades underneath your skin, waiting to emerge. You all have unique powers. You will learn everything you need as you escape and live free. Such it is written; so shall it be." Tears came to his eyes, but his smile never left his face. "The bracelets your mothers gave you will guide you and be a constant companion to help make you aware of everything that is happening around you. Without them, there is nowhere safe for the four of you except Sahael. I must go now, my princesses. I will never forget this moment."

And neither would Oadira. Neither would her sisters. Their

lives had changed forever today. This tent had become their temple; a sacred place of learning that had led them to a greater understanding. Oadira wanted to climb to the top of the colosseum and shout at the top of her lungs. Sahael was real! It wasn't just a story she didn't believe, or a dream she fought to forget. It was real, and so was her power.

Solomon called for Nezikiah, letting him know they had run out of time. They left the tent and made their way back through the catacombs under the arena. The sun had moved toward the horizon as they had learned, turning the sky pink and orange as sunset approached. Eventually they met back up with Madame Lalaurie on one of the battlements where dinner was being served to rich witans in colorful clothing. Silverware clinked against expensive porcelain while light conversation and sycophantic laughter accented the sound of waves on rock below. The madame chuckled embarrassingly as they approached.

"That's a mighty big bull you got there," Lalaurie said. She flipped her hair out of her face and sighed lightly. "We need to set up a schedule of dates and times of when you'll be visiting my family's three estates with your bull."

"A schedule is already in place," Solomon said.

"When's the soonest you can visit the colonies?" Madame Lalaurie asked, eyeing Solomon up and down.

"It is all written here," Solomon said. He handed Lalaurie an envelope with a wax seal. "You'll find the dates to your liking, I'm sure. We will visit your estate first, so have Oadira prepared. We should arrive within days of your return to the plantation. And perhaps while we're there, you and I could get a meal together and discuss future partnerships."

"I would like that very much," Madame Lalaurie sneered. She took a bite of some roasted pork and chewed slowly. "I have another contract that needs to be signed, though, securing the

Lalaurie family's breeding rights."

She took paper and pen from a sheepskin handbag beside the table.

"Are you saying that you want exclusivity to Nezikiah only?" Solomon asked.

"Yes," Madame Lalaurie said.

"That would mean a long-term partnership, as well as further breeding nights with your property."

"It would, but I assure you, the children that will come from these pairings will make us rich beyond your wildest dreams."

"Agreed," Solomon said, shaking Madame Lalaurie's hand.

"See you soon," Madame Lalaurie said as Solomon bowed and winked at the princesses. Nezikiah bowed as well, and the two men left the battlement restaurant.

Oadira hugged her beloved cousins goodbye as the Lalaurie sisters arrived to take them back to their estates. They lingered in their embrace, content in the moment. They had learned more about their heritage and mission in the last few hours than the rest of their lives combined. The future no longer felt unknown and bleak. No matter what happened, they would rise in the morning with new purpose.

"I love you both so much," Oadira whispered into their thoughts. *"I will see you again as free daughters of Sahael on the shores of Alkebulan."*

"We will be free," Heziara agreed.

Aamira nodded. *"Our people will be free as well. I love you."*

As Oadira followed Madame Lalaurie down to the docks and their sleeping quarters for the night, she looked toward the future with hope. Yes, she had to wait a few weeks or months to escape, and her journey from there would be unknown, but free air would soon fill her lungs like the first breath of a newborn child.

One thing she knew for sure: she would never be locked in her room ever again.

TO BE CONTINUED

OUT NOW:

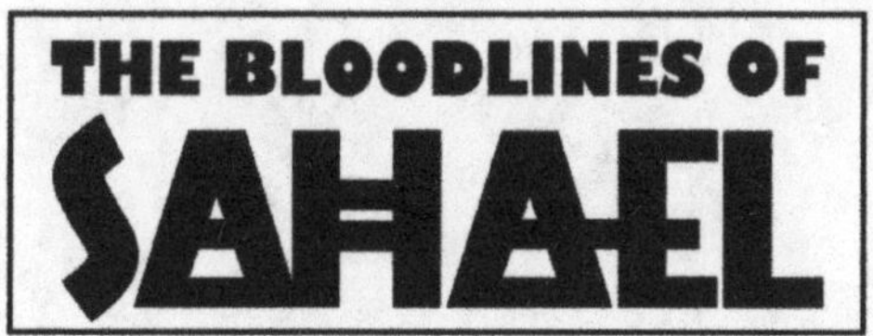

VOLUME ONE

BOOK TWO

THE SECOND SIGN

www.ingramcontent.com/pod-product-compliance
Lightning Source LLC
Chambersburg PA
CBHW010448310726
48979CB00018B/2853/J

* 9 7 8 1 9 6 3 0 8 9 0 0 4 *